CW01278962

Tempest

Tempest

AN ANTHOLOGY

Patrician Press ● Manningtree

First published as a paperback edition by Patrician Press 2019

E-book edition published by Patrician Press 2019

Copyright for Tempest – An Anthology © Patrician Press 2019

Copyright for each text contributed remains with the author

All rights reserved. No part of this document may be reproduced or transmitted in any form or by any means, electronic, mechanical, photocopying, recording, or otherwise, without prior written permission of Patrician Press.

British Library Cataloguing in Publication Data. A catalogue record for this book is available from the British Library.

ISBN paperback edition 978-1-9997030-6-6

TEMPEST AN ANTHOLOGY
EDITED BY ANNA VAUGHT AND ANNA JOHNSON

Published by Patrician Press 2019

For more information: www.patricianpress.com

"The futility of action does not absolve one from the failure to act."
The Last Magician **Janette Turner Hospital**

"...knowledge and sympathy can improve the human condition."
Steven Pinker

"The country is falling apart around us. This is plain even to the pay-no-attention-at-all crowd, even to the low-information undecided-voter segment. It's all crumbling right in front of our eyes." *The Nix* **Nathan Hill**

"Complete freedom for billionaires means poverty, insecurity, pollution and collapsing public services for everyone else. Because we will not vote for this, it can be delivered only through deception and authoritarian control. The choice we face is between unfettered capitalism and democracy. You cannot have both."
George Monbiot

"... some five million women took to the streets in 673 marches worldwide. On seven continents we marched, against Trump and all that he represents: demagoguery, xenophobia, misogyny, racism, sexism, homophobia. Our banners echoed the call of [Sheila Rowbotham's] long-ago rebels, for a future of "liberty, love and solidarity". For most of us, this was the first glimmer of light in a dark time. Hardly utopia, but a moment of genuine hope, born not in some nowhere land of political fantasy but here and now..."
Barbara Taylor

Contents

Anna Vaught
Introduction

When we began planning this anthology, the notion was that it would concern the present political 'tempestuous' times and for a piece of speculative fiction, an exploration in a political parable or elegiac poem or a piece of non-fiction to reflect on our present political problems. I would desist, if I could, from political and social involvement – I know plenty of people who have entirely stopped following the news and/or placed severe limits or careful muting on their social media diet. I understand this, but it is not an option for me or, really, for this press, with its philanthropic bent, passionate sense of questing after social justice and being involved in politics.

Ah, but thereby hangs a tale. I love this book, but I disagree with a number of statements in it. I think that it's partly an intransigent imperviousness to others' ideas which has led us into this present calamity and this book was a lesson to me too; it's not so odd that a book about tempestuous times, about dystopias and visions of the dreadful, should prompt a reader to something different and better. And while the book is a sharing of grief, it is also a conduit to something else.

Our collection begins with Patrick Wright's startling, chilling 1988 account of Trump and Trump Towers, *The Man Who Would be Christ*. It's not long before Christmas and as the author is walking along Fifth Avenue in New York he pauses to look at Trump

Towers. Just inside, its owner is selling something festive, '...an encounter with the man who has already redeveloped Christmas and was now coming forward to reveal his plans for heaven itself.' This is a subtle survey of wealth and morality. Wright asks, 'Is this morality?' (that espoused by Trump), or is it '...just another simulation...?

The Wall by Emma Bamford inventively takes up the notion of Trump's wall and gives it wider scope for the current climate. In this story, British wallers are recruited for the project. This strange dystopian project swings along, until reality bites and a small girl, appearing across the boundary, is threatened, shot at and rescued by her mother. But there's a twist in this tale. A very satisfying one.

The next piece, *Women must act now...* by Ivana Bartoletti, is focused on AI and while the constructs of that are potentially terrifying, its writer is keen to get ahead and work to correct an imbalance and head off some awful things at the pass, when 'the overarching problem of men dictating the rules has found new expression in something that is currently changing the way we live and breathe...' This piece was an eye opener for me; profiling has a long way to go and must be transparent. 'It is time for women not only to investigate what AI means for us, but also to make sure we frame and lead the debate...'

By way of contrast, two poems: *Some start fires* and *Temple for Mithras* by M W Bewick play with tropes of temperature and noise to look at what is lost, what is silenced and what it hurt or suffocated. These are beautiful but chilling pieces. In the first, where 'to be cool, to be cooled, is to be rich', we see comfort as commodity, and we reap our reward as 'firestarters' and careless inhabitants of this planet. The second poem has a contracting, choking urban setting, dystopian again to be sure, with the 'city as relic' where voyages in and out no longer proceed, all dwindles and, I suppose, the spark of the mystery is almost dead. The alliterative 'City of light, concrete and colour' makes me feel a choking as I read it aloud.

But if these two poems set us in a dying world we can just about recognise, then the short story, *This is Earth* by Wersha Bharadwa, takes us to an alien civilisation; to the planet Zerg, where a mother explains the patriarchy and, more specifically rapists, to her baffled daughter – the author is brutally frank in a piece whose uncomfortable humour will surely rattle: 'They've been doing this on planet Earth for millennia.' The girl is going to earth and the mother must prepare her for the place. Of course, we are the aliens and the protagonist of this story is sent to help us, but is scared as she meets men: 'I'd read Earth rapists are mostly guys you know and unless they're registered, there's no way you can identify one.'

The cowboy with the calcium spur by poet Mark Brayley taxes us to reflect on our expectations for our young and on our own fears, '...that simple fear for the future diminishes us all.' The parents who are sure they know best, are faultless and have 'proved just too pampered to permit their own demise.' The child's life is already prescribed, an impulse to correct and organise bound up with the mother's hopes and dreams for her little son. Its vision is moving, tender – and disturbing.

In another poem, the beautiful and mysterious, '*Eclipse*' by Catherine Coldstream, we see a group of people moving on. To where and with whom? Are they stateless? Had they thought they were citizens of the world and thus they are 'citizens of nowhere'? Again, it feels as if life and movement are being commodified at source and, in the process, those who enjoyed those rights, have lost their spirit and remember 'what we'd been told at the outset: take your ticket. Friction./No reaction.'

The poem that follows, *American beauty* by Guy de Cruz, is

angrier; sharper. I imagine someone grieving for our changed knowledge, our skewing of what beauty really is. The eye of that someone sees American magazines; yes, size zero and all the constructs women rightly rail against, but also things that are murderous and 'rot' and 'slaughterhouse taste.' There is something mightily wrong in what we are being peddled and in what we might ingest, unquestioning. Timorous beauty which we should protect is, instead, 'gunned out of its shoe' in this arresting last line.

The walking stick, a short story by Peter Fullagar, looks at a moment, an instant, before 'they' came. It's a response to an imagined dystopian world where we are severely constrained. Doubtful – but then again, is it? Haven't we all seen things that were thought impossible or at least unlikely? – it will be true to life, but shows the possibility of what could happen if we don't all work together.

Save me from the dogs by J L Hall portrays a world which is familiar but askew with 'aurolac and deafening techo and suffocating heat.' It is dangerous to inhale and where a gorgeous natural smell pierces, we discover it is only shower gel. But who are the dogs? Who are 'they'? This is a terrifying world; underground, drug and power-addled, polluted and run by those you should run from, if only you could. Beset by dogs who will ravage you.

From here, it's a hot segue into *Rage* by Sam Jordison, which expresses how many of us are feeling. While Sam's piece is not only about Brexit, I feel the same sensations clearly and know that they are not always good for my health. 'I'm trying to remember the last time I went through twenty four hours without feeling angry.' Me too. 'I'm writing this in June 2018 and it feels like we're falling.' Doesn't it? We are chasing our tails, 'Like everyone else.'

The immediate fury of Sam's piece is quite a contrast with short story, *A tasty morsel* by Emma Kittle-Pey, which seems to begin with the wholesome entities of making compost and prepping your bake for the PTA cake sale. But from here it quickly darkens because, underneath the pleasure of baking, is a treacherous set of elements and people too. The sea here is real – a beautiful thing that, even in the smallest cascade of tempest, will kill you – and an extended metaphor for what lies beneath.

In *The carp whisperer* by Petra McQueen and Katy Wimhurst, the pulse of water and the freedom it connotes acts a counterpoint to images of stale confinement and of oppression; here, citizens – with their lives' accoutrements – are bracketed into classes: the categorisation of individuals is haunting. This is a beautiful story but it reminds me of things that break my heart. And yet, there is an impulse of hope here: '*We are water. We are life.*'

Populists are on the rise by Chantal Mouffe is an arresting, unsettling piece. Consider her summary at the beginning: 'Neoliberalism has created genuine grievances, exploited by the radical right. The left must find a new way to articulate them.' Mouffe unpicks the things that have come apart in our politics and in our democracies and it is tragic. And yet, as she tackles the different political strategies, she sees that this might also be a time of recreative energy if we could make the apparatus to go forward. She cites recent examples where if 'an egalitarian discourse is available to express their grievances, many people join the progressive struggle.' I hope so.

Fenner by Suzy Norman is chilling in a different way. Time is tight, weather is biting, loss is keenly felt. There are pretty but melancholy splashes of 'Under Milk Wood' in the darkness here, in the vestiges of memory in the old gothic house, where 'The pipes howl with life and the roof sags above my head.' Perhaps promising a new life of uncertain good.

The flotsam boy by Steven O'Brien: here, we are at the sea again, combining what is beautiful and loving and the shocking notion of the loss of a single child. In the story, the author surrounds the child with a kind sea and the wishes of an old man who finds him. With spells and love, he is awakened and it's almost unbearable. The boy is not anonymous: he is celebrated and he has a voice, listened to tenderly: 'Try to find his family and if you cannot find them, watch over him until he grows to be a man.' Every reader will see a particular child in this.

In *Nature and culture* by Jules Pretty, one is invited to keep watch too. This time, over nature and biodiversity. But it's more than that because, as Pretty explores here, 'the diversity of life involves both the living forms (biological diversity) and the worldviews and cosmologies of what life means (cultural diversity).' It's fascinating to work through the author's ideas on how different cultures may view nature, but of course, underlying one culture's 'biophilia' is the potential for threat, dystopia and destruction; without 'ecological literacy' we risk so much.

The next piece in the anthology, *Bethlehem 16th May 2018* by Mazin Qumsiyeh is shocking, necessarily so; its first lines: 'I write from Bethlehem, where 200,000 Palestinians have been squeezed into a canton, a ghetto, a *bantustan* or an open-air prison...' This piece is a passionate dissection of injustice, 'false Gods' and propaganda; it is a dissection of falsification and a blow to the head if you were, in any way, suffering from complacency that the events it describes were not happening now. Qumsiya's piece demands of its reader an urgent reading of 'stolen lands' and of a 'violation of international law.'

The job by Martin Reed may make you shift your feet unsteadily, moving, worrying along, between the avatar and the real; the 'ownworld' and the real world; between what is credible and what is not; between what is explicit and what is rather more insidious in its control, with its 'plugins' and strange virtual world. It's all about control and the striking – almost funny – ending creeps up on you because, 'There's a title that goes with... the job.'

It's a neat movement from here to *A narrow escape for the Chelsea Hotel* by Robert Ronsson because of that title. Now, we are in 1978, watching a 'bustling young property developer.' He's brash, he's supremely confident and he *wants things*. Such as this place. It could be, 'A classy hotel.' He's keen to make it beautiful, his own, expunge the traces, perhaps, of Sid and Nancy. But the hotel is not for sale. Isn't it though? It's a terrible thought: that everything and everyone *is*: here's what's at the heart of this particular dystopia.

'*We should own the stars*': *Postcapitalism, Techno-Utopianism and Blade Runner 2049* by Sean Seeger looks at the role of technological advances in our future. The writer tangles with testy concepts such as 'fully automated luxury communism' and – it is frightening to many – whether developments spell doom (an 'unparalleled extension of the apparatus of human control') or something altogether more positive in liberating people from 'material scarcity.' There are questions the film *Blade Runner* leaves us with: 'that of how the coming technologies might be made to enrich human life and serve collective ends, as opposed to intensifying existing patterns of inequality, exploitation, and ecological devastation.'

There's more sea, more water in *Tempest on Tyneside* by Justine Sless and there are humorous shades of Shakespeare's *The Tempest* here, too. In this story, the influx of people is from South to North because they are in search of beer, and tempers are frayed. There are mighty storms and bits from a sign advertising tours to 'Buckingham Palace'; underneath the feet of the influx and the residents, there is a fault line and it's moving. 'I've seen storms rage for years now and I always think that it can get no worse...' Yet, as the wall of encroaching water subsides, the game kicks off in the 'stadium of light.' You would think that life could not continue, so tempest-tossed. Somehow it does. It clings on.

'The sea like the wind was all around us' is the epigraph to *On Boredom Isle* by Elisa Marcella Webb. Here, in this empty land, dying of boredom, and – horribly – with a dying sister to whom no warmth seems to be expressed, the protagonist writes 'S K E L E T A L' on the sand because it's a good word. She hopes for something dreadful to happen just so there's an event. It's not only rabid, hideous activity that's a dystopia; it's also the absence of the vital or the numinous – such as in this place, where 'The window gazed out to sea, even the room wanted to escape.' The very fabric of the place is stultified and smothered.

Do let us know what you think of and how you are affected by any of the pieces here. During this tempest may I, as editor, perhaps baffling and battering you with the contents of this anthology, still show an affirming flame. You may call me naïve, but I maintain: *it is not too late.*

The man who would be Christ

Patrick Wright

About six months ago, I was in New York City for a brief visit and took a walk up Fifth Avenue one Sunday before Christmas. The street was packed with shoppers and the Salvation Army were well dug in on the corners, tinkling handbells against the noise of blaring car horns, and foraying out into the crowd to appeal on behalf of the unfortunates for whom Christmas promised only another freezing night in a doorway.

The shop windows were alight with seasonal tableaux. The larger department stores had roped off special viewing areas on the street, put their doormen out as ushers and filled their windows with animated dream sequences m which Christmas merged with peak moments in the history of the American spirit.

The real crowd-puller was set in a nursery interior of the most wishful old-fashioned kind. A model steam train circled a laden Christmas tree and then wound through the cuttings and tunnels of a snow-covered landscape in the next window. Around the train model children went through mechanical motions of their own: fixing a broken carriage, working the controls or just following things with an enchanted doe-like eye. Saks and Co may deal in the latest styles, but the sentimentally contrived clockwork romance in their window greeted every passing shopper as Citizen Kane.

Further along Fifth Avenue I came to a new building which is a stranger to such discretion. Identified by two-foot high bronze letters over its prominent doorway, this is Trump Tower – an uncompromisingly modern glass edifice which rises in stepped and tree-covered terraces up to the height of the Tiffany building next door, and then soars on up for 58 saw-toothed floors.

Trump Tower is unmistakably brazen. Huge revolving doors deliver one, under the watchful eye of doormen whose uniforms have been likened to those of South American generals on parade, into an 'atrium' of bursting flamboyance. The place is an explosion of polished brass and brilliant pink marble – raised to a high shine on both floor and walls. Reflective glass fills the area with a speculative sense of space and escalators rise up one side of the atrium, doubling people with their own reflections and moving the whole preoccupied assemblage up and down between five floors of exclusive shops: Asprey, Buccellati, Cartier, Charles Jourdan, Bonwit Teller. . . The atrium converges on an impressive monument to liquidity, through-put and flow – an amber-lit waterfall tumbles down 80 feet of soapy pink marble and then sits bubbling in the bistro.

Just inside those revolving doors the Trump Tower was offering something truly unique: an encounter with the man who has already redeveloped Christmas and was now coming forward to reveal his plans for Heaven itself. A monstrous neo-baroque table had been isolated behind burgundy velvet ropes. It stood there motionless, while its legs crawled with busty gilt figurines. Behind the table sat a blow-dried Trump, looking impassive in a pink silk tie and a long dark blue coat. Next to him a woman was selling copies of a book, taking them from a big pile behind her and cranking away with an American Express machine. Three tall and immaculately tonsured black dudes were in attendance; dressed in charcoal suits, they were supervising the queuing crowd and keeping an eye out for assassins. Trump was settled into his chosen version of clockwork routine: leaning forward to ask the name of each approaching supplicant, and then falling back to write a dedication in felt-tip scrawl.

There was Donald Trump as image on the cover of his just-published book: 60 floors up with Central Park behind him and his name overhead in the largest gold letters that Random House could find. Here was Donald Trump incarnate: selling the word to his disciples while a brassy version of 'Oh Come All Ye Faithful' poured from the sound system and filled the thronging atrium behind.

It would indeed be a churlish visitor who stepped into Donald Trump's atrium and refused to marvel. In stark contrast with British endeavours like the Trocadero near Piccadilly Circus, Trump Tower demonstrates that a building can be glitzy without also being tacky. Ike Turner should take heart. Cruelly lampooned as the man whose front room proved that it really was possible to spend a million dollars in Woolworths, he can now visit Trump Tower and stand assured that the problem was never just a matter of taste. Quantity can be both piled up and transmuted into quality. Towering and significant structures can be built up entirely from clichés. Hailed and deplored as the building which brought the vulgarity of Las Vegas and Atlantic City to Manhattan, Trump Tower is also dedicated to the televisual opulence of *Dallas* and *Dynasty*. Indeed, the atrium was quickly adopted as a location for the next generation of soaps. The CBS mini-series, *I'll Take Manhattan*, didn't just take its cameras into the bistro. It took Trump and gave him a part.

Opening their personalised first editions of *Trump: The Art of the Deal* on their way home, Donald Trump's followers will have discovered that the man who has recently been feted as 'America's masterbuilder' is not moved by lust for money alone: 'I've got enough, much more than I'll ever need.' The animating impulse is of a grander and more worthy kind. Where others 'paint beautifully on canvas or write wonderful poetry', Trump likes 'making deals, preferably big deals. That's how I get my kicks.'

As an artist of the deal, Trump takes a distinctive approach to his work. He likes each day to resemble his retail atrium: an unpredicted 'happening', as he once described it, which declares its own unique prospects as it goes along. Not a man to weigh himself down with a brief case, he is equally careful to avoid stifling the creative play of his imagination with 'structure' of a bureaucratic kind. Confident in his own sense of what it is to be a developer, Trump likes 'to come to work each day and just see what develops'. He styles himself somewhere between a Zen master and Jackson Pollock, who talked famously of the things that happen 'when I am in my painting'. Like other artists Trump has his chosen medium; the day starts to move at about nine in the morning when 'I get on the phone'.

His book offers the inside story on Trump Tower. As Trump writes, 'a guy named Arthur Drexler, from the Museum of Modern Art, put it very well when he said 'Skyscrapers are machines for making money'. Drexler meant it as a criticism. I saw it as an incentive.' While architecture critics carped on about aesthetics, Trump knew that he was in the fantasy business. After 'assembling' his site and winning every possible planning concession, he focused everything on his chosen market. He set out to create a building with 'aura' – one that was 'larger than life' and would appeal to 'the wealthy Italian with the beautiful wife and the red Ferrari'.

False economies were out. Whether or not Trump was really targeting the mafia, the idea was to make people feel 'comfortable, but also pumped up to spend money'. If customers would enjoy the massage of being taken for a ride on solid-bronze escalators, then Trump wasn't going to scrimp on the million dollars this extra touch cost. If they would be more turned on by two million dollars' worth of purling waterfall than by the conventional 'art' suggested by various unimaginative advisers, then this, too, would be part of the deal. As for all that soapy pink marble, the name is *Breccia Pernice* and Trump recalls the day when he and his wife first saw a sample of this rare stone – an 'exquisite blend of rose, peach, and pink that literally took our breath away'. The transports turned out to be mutual. With Trump rejecting 60 per cent of the stone that was cut because of white streaks that were 'jarring to me', the top of an Italian mountain had been removed before the floors and walls of the retail atrium were clad to their creator's satisfaction.

Trump: The Art of the Deal is a high-rise autobiography of the increasingly familiar co-written type. It tells the tale of a man who lives on the 58th floor and is still going up. Donald Trump was born a few million dollars up from the ground floor, but he is at pains to point out that he still started his ascent from a proper home. His father is Fred Trump, a tough developer of low-cost working-class housing who has made his packet in outer New York boroughs like Queens and the Bronx. By the forties when Donald was just an infant, Fred Trump was borrowing millions from the Federal Housing Administration to build high-rise apartment complexes, and then bringing in controversial 'windfall profits' by forcing the projects through under budget.

Donald doesn't dwell on the various scandals that attended his father's successful exploitation of public funds, preferring to recall the family home as a 'very traditional' place. Fred is featured as 'the power and breadwinner' while Mary, his Scottish spouse, glows in her son's memory as 'the perfect housewife' who loved her children, darned socks and did charity work. Church was on Fifth Avenue where the Trump family would go to hear the message from Norman Vincent Peale, a minister who was also the best-selling author of *The Power of Positive Thinking*. School was a Military Academy in upstate New York. Donald's favourite among the teachers was 'a former drill sergeant in the marines' whose educational method was to 'go for the jugular' whenever he sensed weakness.

Young Donald made his first big deal while still at college. He bought Swifton Village, a housing project in Cincinnati which had run into trouble, at a knock-down price and wasted no time in getting rid of the hillbilly tenants who had drifted in from Kentucky and turned the place into a slum. He then fixed it up 'to attract a better element', adding shutters and colonial style doors before cranking up the rents. The final touch was to sell the whole thing to a well-lunched sucker from an out-of-town investment trust just as the area was nose diving.

Trump was still in his twenties when he decided to bring his artistry to bear on Manhattan itself. While still at business school he had talked ambitiously about changing the Manhattan skyline, and in 1971 he rented a bachelor apartment on Third Avenue and started to 'walk the streets' in search of likely properties. He also finessed his way into exclusive clubs where he would enjoy dating 'the most beautiful women in the world' and worrying paunchy grey-haired husbands with his own lean good looks. From here the story is one of unchecked ascent and it involves what Trump, remembering his old baseball coach, calls 'leverage' as well as the more conventional strengths of tooth and nail. There are the lawsuits, there are the contributions to politicians, there are the first sites picked out among the welfare hotels and drug-infested parks of Manhattan's more blighted areas, and bought at a knock-down price when New York City was slumped.

One deal leads to the next, but as Donald Trump rises up

through a growing empire of abandoned railyards, hotels, casinos and apartment buildings overlooking Central Park, his story diversifies beyond its catalogue of accumulations. There are the rewards: the helicopters, yachts and jet planes, the meetings with famous men (from John Cardinal O'Connor to Jimmy Carter and Ronald Reagan), the fabulous houses and, of course, the superb wife. As a Czech who possesses the physical prowess of an Olympic skier, the looks of a former 'top-model' and the conventional wifely virtues of homeliness and motherhood, Ivana Trump is portrayed as a perfect partner for the man who can take his pick.

At the heart of Trump's story is a drama of struggle. Trump has come into conflict with a variety of forces: architectural preservationists who have resisted his demolition crews, community boards which have fought his planning applications, well-off people who are enjoying rent-controlled or rent-stabilised tenancies in apartment buildings which Trump wants to tear down, journalists who have dared to criticise, bureaucrats who have used public authority to stand in his way. Recalling the outcry that met his plan to bury the old Commodore Hotel under curtain walls of reflective glass, Trump is pleased to point out that in transforming the hotel into the Grand Hyatt he has 'created four walls of mirrors' that, far from failing to fit in, make the surrounding traditional buildings more visible than ever.

The battle of the Bonwit Teller murals is less easily settled. While demolishing the old Bonwit building to make way for Trump Tower, Donald found that it would be unexpectedly expensive to remove the Art Deco friezes that he had agreed to give to the Metropolitan Museum of Art. So, as he writes, 'I ordered my guys to rip them down'. There was considerable public outcry and while Trump insists (with all the confidence of a true artist) that the murals were overrated and that many of his critics were 'phonies and hypocrites', he also confesses to slight feelings of regret.

Worse problems were to come at 100 Central Park South when Trump hired Citadel Management to run the building in a way that would encourage tenants to leave and suggested, with what many recognised as a shocking degree of cynicism, that the apartments that were already vacant might be used to house New York's homeless.

There are other stories that Trump prefers to leave out. There is no mention here of Paul Gapp, architecture critic of the *Chicago Tribune* who described one of Trump's towering schemes as 'architecturally lousy' and was promptly (and unsuccessfully) sued for $500 million. There is no mention of Eddie and Julius Trump who were sued for using their own name in business ('I would like them to change their name', Donald Trump remarked of this unrelated pair whose 'Trump Group' had been established for 20 years). Neither is there any word of Alvin Gunther, the man who was killed by a shard of glass which fell from the heights of Trump Tower on the day of its opening in 1983.

Trump likes to project himself as a champion of the underdog pitched against an all-powerful establishment – whether he is hiring as many women as possible into top positions in his organisation or taking on his own tenants. In 1986, he adopted the case of Mrs Annabel Hill, an 'adorable little lady from Georgia' who was about to lose her farm through mortgage foreclosure. Mrs Hill's 67-year-old husband had already committed suicide in the vain hope that insurance money would settle the debt. She was still $100,000 short when Trump launched the appeal that would finally set her free. On 23 December 1986 there had been another innovative Christmas performance in the retail atrium of Trump Tower: a mortgage burning ceremony in which Trump held the paper while a grateful Mrs Annabel Hill applied the flame.

Trump's most successful engagement with the establishment has been his dog-fight with Ed Koch, the mayor of New York. Trump harps on a popular chord when he denounces Koch as a bully, moron and coward whose administration is both 'pervasively corrupt and totally incompetent'. Trump 'beat the hell' out of Koch in getting a tax-abatement to build his Tower, and he then found the perfect opportunity to prove his charge of incompetence. In June 1980 the City authorities closed the Wollman Skating Rink in Central Park, intending to rebuild it over two years. Six years of bungling and 12 million squandered dollars later, New York City officials announced their decision to start the rebuilding all over again. It was then that Trump made his move, offering to finance and build a brand new ice-rink on the Wollman site in six months, on the condition that he could lease the rink from the city at a 'fair market rental'. Trump finished the job and the Wollman story became one of the national events of the year. Trump offers it as a modern parable: 'It was a simple, accessible drama about the contrast between governmental incompetence and the power of effective private enterprise.'

By this time Trump has brought his gasping readers up those 58 floors. They've rubbed shoulders with Trump Tower's exclusive residents: the wealthy French people who came here to sit out the Mitterrand years; the Asians and Arabs who couldn't get through the discriminatory vetting procedures of the cooperatives that control so many of New York's most exclusive apartment buildings; stars like Steven Spielberg, Johnny Carson, Paul Anka and the now deceased Liberace. Having raised his readers up this high, Donald Trump offers them the ultimate Christmas tableau: a fleeting glimpse into the enchanted world of America's loudest billionaire.

The Trumps' New York home is a million dollar triplex at the very top of the Tower. Visiting the Saudi billionaire Adnan

Khashoggi in Olympic Tower one day in 1985, Trump found himself in 'the biggest living room I'd ever seen' and decided that he'd quite like one of his own. 'What the hell,' he thought to himself, 'Why shouldn't I have exactly the apartment I wanted – particularly when I built the whole building?' So Trump stands there and gestures toward the 27 solid marble columns which Italy's finest craftsmen carved for his 80 foot living room, announcing that 'they arrived yesterday, and they're beautiful'. Lest anyone should have missed the point, he rubs it in: 'What I'm doing is about as close as you're going to get, in the twentieth century, to the quality of Versailles.'

As we take our privileged glimpse into this celestial place, a curious kind of morality play rolls into action. The first scenes are of unchecked extravagance, hedonism and luxury, but it is not long before an alarming giddiness sets in. The pleasures of megalomania should not be underestimated, but it can still be hard to live so far beyond the limits of the normal human condition: everything about oneself – every utterance, every passing thought, every memory – starts to burn with intense significance and before long gravity itself gives way. Even such a distinguished artist of the deal as Donald Trump is susceptible to vertigo so, like Harold with his Purple Crayon in that much-loved American children's story from the fifties, he no sooner finds himself in thin air than he quickly sketches in some firm ground under his feet.

If Trump was in the White House, which, as he hints, he may well be before too long, he might follow the example of President Reagan and look for astrological anchorage in the stars. But his Christmas tableau is actually more like an old-fashioned western than a story of special people with occult powers. Trump styles himself and his friends as real men who have carved their initials into the world's most famous skyline. Their Manhattan penthouses become tents on the high plains of America's last frontier. They sit at the fireside, remembering Mother and distinguishing themselves from the lesser types who continually get in their way. As real men of action, these fellows of the deal know that you've 'got to take a stand or people will walk all over you'. They have as little regard for 'suckers' as they do for 'employees'. In their book, an 'employee' is either a woman or a eunuch who 'thinks small'.

Trump's true companions of the deal defend simple 'gut-feeling' in a world full of spurious specialisation and bureaucratic procedure. As men of unlimited wealth and power, they continue to think of themselves as underdogs oppressed by an unaccountable establishment. They see con-men and bullshit everywhere. Between themselves, however, there is a code of honour. Like true *mafiosi,* they know that 'you can trust family in a way that you can never trust anyone else'. They also know that sometimes it is more important to 'pay your respects' than to make money, so they will pass up a promising deal to get to the funeral of a much respected 'patriarch'.

The companions of the deal may not understand all the technicalities, but they know that a handshake is the sign of a man's word, and have nothing but contempt for the 'low-lifes, the horror-shows' for whom only the signed contract counts.

This is how Trump finally styles himself: a man who has broken all the limits but who has also reinvented morality. He has everything the world can offer but, as he likes to point out, he has never touched a drop of alcohol or smoked a cigarette in his life. A man who got married in the church of his childhood and who has gone on to stand tall as a true patriarch in his own family, Trump is also a man of charity who has done his bit for the Vietnam Veterans and other worthy causes. Indeed, he is even moral in his egotism. Some people may jeer as he tries to write his name in large bronze letters over the world but, as he has replied, at least he has a reputation to uphold – unlike the sharks who hide their real identity under anonymous company titles.

Is this morality just another simulation, like the clockwork display just down the road in Saks and Co's window? It's hard for an outsider to say with any certainty. There can be little doubt, however, that morality, like money, is something the rich need far more of than the rest of us.

(Published in New Statesman and Society, 17 June 1988, pp. 35-38)

The wall

Emma Bamford

Evening, David. Graham. How's your lad, Joe? Doing better? Glad to hear it. Ah, that's better. Good to take the weight off. Evening, Fiona. Pint of the usual please. Thanks. Can you take out what you need from that? I've come straight from the field, haven't got my glasses with me. Do you need another 20p? Might have one somewhere in my pocket. Yes, there we go. Grand.

What's that, Drew? Ah, come off it. I'm sure you don't want to hear me rambling on about all that again. Surely you're tired of hearing about it? I know you are, Simon. Must've told you a thousand times by now. Really, Drew? How'd you miss it? Ah yes, I forgot you'd been away. Come off it, you're not wanting to hear all that. It's long past. You know me – not much of a one for the television or the newspapers. Got plenty to be getting on with without all that.

Lord, can't a man get a bit of peace with his pint of an evening after a hard day's labour? If I tell you, will you leave me be? Yes? All right then.

It started with a letter. Don't get many letters these days, apart from bills, you know. Seems everyone's given up on writing. Too busy sending these e-mails and text messages and what have you.

Not got to grips with all that myself. Don't see that need for it. What's wrong with a good old fashioned conversation? I know, Joe, I agree.

Anyway, I come in one evening. Been up the Hatwick farm. Big job, that one. So I get home and there's a letter on the doormat. Big, it is, so as I know it's not a bill. Thick envelope. Cream coloured. Funny postmark. I pick it up and put it on the kitchen table, to open later, while I'm having my tea. Oh, I can't remember. What does it matter what I had? Sausages maybe. A pie. The usual. Trust you to be thinking about your stomach, Joe. Too right, it's big enough!

So I'm eating my sausages – or my pie, or what not – and after I've finished with my knife I use it to open the envelope. There's a letter inside, official-looking. It takes me a while to find my glasses and when I get them on and pick up the letter again, I'm astonished to see it comes from the American government. I'm blowed if I know what that's all about. There must have been a mistake, I think to myself. I've never been to America in my life, not even left England, apart from that one trip to Cardiff back in '87. Haven't got a passport. They must have mixed me up with someone else, sent me their parking tickets or whatever it is. I look at the envelope again. No clues there. I start to read the letter. 'Dear Mr Nettleship,' it says.

I'm starting to think it's a trick: someone's printed this off the internet and sent it to me as some kind of practical joke, but turns out it's real. From the US Customs and Border Protection. The newly formed Construction Department. Looking for wallers, wanting them to work on a big project. Says they'll pay travel and a good wage, too.

Ah, thanks Fiona. Drew's paying.

Happen it were the monthly meeting of our our group that night anyway. Ah, you're a one, Drew. Not Alcoholics

Anonymous, no. The local branch of the Association of Master Wallers. Been a member thirty year. Youngest in the county to be asked to join, I were. Being the son of a waller and the grandson of a waller, it's in my blood. Never thought of doing anything else. Course, when I were young I thought I could change the world. But a bit of hard work soon knocked that thought out of me. What difference can a waller make to anything, me dad said. And I listened.

Well, I get to the meeting and all of us have had one of these letters. There's a bit of a to-do about it and then someone raises a motion and we all have a debate and a vote. As you know, I'm not a political man, me. Not got much time for politicians and the like. Never seems to make much difference, it's usually a lot of hot air then nothing changes. But I've always done my civic duty, voted all my life, same way my dad did and the same way as his dad did before him. Both for government and with the wallers. And I stand by what I pledge. So we have our ballot and the motion is carried and that's that. Before I know it I've got a passport in my hand. Imagine! At my age!

Can't say I understand what all the fuss is about, with aeroplanes. People jetting off here, there and everywhere on foreign holidays. Seen cattle treated better. We get off the first plane and onto another – even smaller, this one – and then it's onto an army bus and off we go, for fifty mile or so. My God, it were hot. They take us to this little town called Esperanza in Texas. I know. I thought that, too. But no, it were just over the border, in America. Exactly like a town from a Western, it were. Flat roofs. Not much of anything other than a bar, a general store, petrol station (except they call it a gas station). Even saw some of that – what do you call it? Tumbleweed. They show us our digs for the month. There's a few of us. They put us up in the hotel.

Nothing fancy but it does us okay. You should have seen the size of the breakfasts.

In the morning we get back on the bus and they drive us to the site and explain the job. We each have a section assigned, they say, to be near a hundred foot long and thirty high. In total it is to stretch 2,000 mile, they say, from the Pacific coast to the Atlantic. Each section will join to the next, clicking together like a string of pearls until it stretches right across the country. Wallers from different countries are to build in their native style. Us English are all together – I heard that abutting our section were a bit being built by Italians and, on the far side, some from Kazakhstan. Do you know they still make their bricks out of mud? Just chuck it in a mould and let it harden in the sun, apparently. No need for firing.

The official looking chappy giving us our instructions starts to talk about things like cohesion and unity and, I'll be honest with you, I did start to drift off. It's not for me to question why they have to bring in labour from other countries or why they don't have enough skilled workers themselves to do it. Who knows? Maybe they were just trying to get it done quick. Biggest since the Great Wall of China. That's quite a task.

Sure, I'll take another pint, Joe. Thanks. Very generous.

Of course, why someone wants to build a wall is not for me to question. I'm just there to do the best I can. Five generations of wallers there's been in my family. Five. It's in the blood. And at the end of the day, a wall is a wall, quoin to quoin, course layered after course, pins and ties, all the way up to the cope.

This wall is to be taller than that any of us have built before and so we have between us a bit of a confab, to work out the best way to go about it. And once we're settled, each man sets to his task, and that's that.

Near a month we work, picked up early morning by the bus, dropped back again in the evening, tired as owt. I'll say this for the

Yanks, they feed you well. Steaks the like of which I've never seen before and not likely to see again.

Day after day is pretty much the same, except this one time, when I feel someone's eyes on me and I look up and there's a little dark-haired girl, in a grubby dress, staring at me. Couldn't have been more than eighty feet away, out in the sun-baked dirt. After a bit I give her a wave and she doesn't do anything, just stands there. Got no shoes on. Probably about eight years old. Reminded me of our Lydia, when she were that age. Then one of the officials – a guard, this one – must've noticed me looking because he marches over to me and calls something over to the lass, in another language. Spanish, presumably. I can't tell what he's saying but it's clear from his tone he's ordering her off.

The girl stops where she is, just looking. She's not doing any harm and she's close enough that I can see dust smears on her legs. Funny place to play, I think, so far away from anywhere, and while I'm pondering on that the guard raises his voice at her, and still she's standing there and then he's shouting the same thing over and over, getting louder, and now he raises his gun and I hear an awful click as he swings it up and onto his shoulder, taking aim at her through the sight, and it's as if everything suddenly stops. No sounds. No movement. And then I see a woman come from somewhere, from behind a rock or I don't know where, and she runs towards the girl, silently, and swoops her up and turns and runs and runs, not screaming or saying anything, that gun trained on them until they're too far away to see and I'm finally able to look at the guard, just feet away from me, and he lowers his gun slowly, wipes his sleeve across his brow, spits onto the earth. Later I realise the woman's left her bags behind, just dropped them in the dust. They stay there, these bags, for the next few days, and I wonder to myself what's in them – food? Clothes? The girl's toys?

– and I keep thinking about it until I've built my section so high I can't see them no more.

A few days after, another government official comes to see us, while we're out working. I wonder if the girl is what he's come to talk about but no – the wall is almost complete, he says, and as we're right in the middle of the country he has news for us: the president himself is going to come to inspect the wall, and they're going to do a special ceremony, and invite the world's press, and the president'll lay the final stone, put on a show for the cameras.

Now you know me, I'm not much of a one for pomp and ceremony. Never sought the limelight, not like some round here I could mention, hey? But it seems I have no choice. They give us instructions on what we have to do, where we have to stand, and they tell us not to tell anyone that he's coming.

Next morning we're there nice and early and they position us in front of a big pile of stones. Limestone, what we'd been working with the past few weeks. They'd sourced decent stones, I'll give them that. Good quality. Very suitable for the task.

Standing there a long time, in neat lines, there must be a hundred of us. It's a hot morning, hot and dry, and I can feel the sweat starting to trickle down my forehead. They've put up some low steel barriers to hold back the reporters and the photographers because there are so many of them and it hits me – this is going to go out to the whole world. Then it's like a ripple goes through the crowd and they snap to attention. The plastic-metallic clicks as they all turn to point their cameras in the same direction reminds me of that guard taking aim at that girl.

There's a cavalcade coming down the road, limousines and outriders, police cars flashing red and blue, and in a whirl of dust it comes to a stop not far from where we wait. The press men and women all surge forward, jostling for position, a hundred arms clutching microphones extending past the metal barrier, and then car doors are opened and person after person after person gets out, all very formal and dressed in suits.

I'll tell you this: he's smaller than he looks on the telly. And his missus – nothing on her moved. Not a hair, not the hem of her skirt, not her lips. Solid she were. Like the rocks of our wall.

We'd done a good job with that wall, if I do say so myself. Course, a well-built dry stone wall will stand for centuries. Some are still going from Old Testament times. Vegetation's your biggest worry, creeping in and weakening things, but not in an arid place like this, in Esperanza, Texas. You build a proper dry stone wall in a place like this and it'll last, that's for sure.

The president goes forward to a lectern someone has put out, between us and the press. And as he gives his speech he's got his back to us, so we can't hear him very well. Mind, I don't think that even if he'd been facing me I would have been able to concentrate any better on what he were saying because a) we've got a barrage of cameras and the full force of the world's gaze directed at us now, and b) I'm trying to run through in my head exactly what it is I have to do when he's finished speaking; how they instructed us yesterday and what, as a group of wallers, we'd rehearsed last night back at the hotel.

Then it's time, and he moves away from the lectern and one of the press advisers holds out an arm to guide him towards us and he's coming our way and I know it's my turn. Yesterday, I'd been told – briefed, they call it – that I had to step forward and hand the president the final stone to lay. I'm not to say a word, just hand it over and show him where to place it. And then the wall'll be complete. So I do as I'm meant to, nervous as anything, I'll admit, and I step forward, and hand him the stone. He grins at the cameras and says, 'I promised that I would build this wall, to make sure America and all Americans are safe,' and then he turns to the wall to fit the final stone.

It won't fit, of course. I've chosen one that's slightly too large. Not obviously so, just a bit, so he has to spend a couple of seconds tilting it this way and that, thinking it will go, somehow, trying to get it to slot into place, like he's doing a jigsaw. No matter what he tries, though, he's not going to be able to get it in. I've made sure of that.

But the distraction is just enough that the rest of us wallers get our chance, and we all step forward, surrounding him, stones in our grip, and we wall, faster than we've ever walled before, moving so quickly that our hands are a blur as we work, layering and building. We're past his waist before he realises what's going on, then up to his shoulders before he has the chance to shout out to his security – although what are they going to do? They can't shoot us, not with all them cameras recording what's going on.

We're beyond his head in the blink of an eye. I lay the final capstone on and others are ready with their hammers to knock in the pebbles. There's one last final tap to lock everything in place and then that's it, job done. The wall is finished.

Women must act now...

Ivana Bartoletti

Women must act now, or male-designed robots will take over our lives

Algorithms are displaying white male bias, and automation is decimating our jobs – we have a lot to lose unless we get involved.

The overarching problem of men dictating the rules has found new expression in something that is currently changing the way we live and breathe: artificial intelligence (AI).

Let us be clear. There are great benefits in the use of AI and we should cherish them. However, the issue is not innovation, or the pace of technological improvement. The real problem is the governance of AI, the ethics underpinning it, the boundaries we give it and, within that, who is going to define all those.

With that in mind, I think the next fight for us women is to ensure artificial intelligence does not become the ultimate expression of masculinity.

There are many reasons to fear this could happen. First, the algorithms that codify human choices about how decisions should be made. It is not possible for algorithms to remain immune from the human values of their creators. If a non-diverse workforce is creating them, they are more prone to be implanted with unexamined, undiscussed, often unconscious assumptions and biases about things such as race, gender and class. What if the workforce designing those algorithms is male-dominated? This is the first major problem: the lack of female scientists and, even worse, the lack of true intersectional thinking behind the creation of algorithms.

Examples of bias were reported by the Guardian a few years back, showing that searching Google for the phrase 'unprofessional hairstyles for work' led to images of mainly black women with natural hair, while searching for 'professional hairstyles' offered pictures of coiffed white women. Or take Microsoft's Tay chatbot, which was created to strike up conversations with millennials on Twitter. The algorithm had been designed to learn how to mimic others by copying their speech. But within 24 hours of being online, it had been led astray, and became a genocide-supporting, anti-feminist Nazi, tweeting messages such as: 'Hitler did nothing wrong.'

What can we do about it? Obviously, encouraging more women to take up the profession and create algorithms would be a great step forward, and we are still lagging behind on this. However, we also need to start querying the outcomes of the decisions made by algorithms and demand transparency in the process that leads to them. Although the new EU General Data Protection Regulation does not go far enough, it does broaden the definition of profiling activities, thus providing us with tools to avoid profiling-based decisions by questioning them. There are no legal certainties yet about how far the new European regulations, which come into force on 25 May, can be taken, but pressure must be applied to ensure AI algorithms are not just powerful and scalable but also transparent to inspection.

Of course, the problem of AI goes beyond this. Some academics, such as Joanna Bryson and Luciano Floridi, argue that AI companies should be regulated like architects, who learn to work with city planners, certification schemes and licences to make buildings safe. They argue for watchdogs and regulators.

It is encouraging that in the UK the government has set up the Centre for Data Ethics. This new body is tasked with advising on the measures needed to enable and ensure safe, ethical and innovative uses of data-driven technologies. Tech UK, which represents the tech industry, is also having conversations on the subject. For the feminist movement, the challenge is to frame the debate and not to let others decide for us.

And let's not forget the impact on the labour market, with women projected to take the biggest hit to jobs in the near future as a result of automation replacing human activities, according to the World Economic Forum. Women are more likely to be employed in jobs that face the highest automation risks. For example, 73% of cashiers in shops are women and 97% of cashiers are expected to lose their jobs to automation. The same report predicts that persistent gender gaps in science, technology, engineering and mathematics (Stem) fields over the next 15 years will also undermine women's professional presence.

And if robots are taking human jobs, we need to figure out how we would deal with a large jobless population. Bill Gates believes that governments should tax companies' use of robots, as a way to at least temporarily slow the spread of automation and to fund other types of employment. And many now suggest that universal basic income is probably the only solution to the rise of robotic automation. This is appealing to many but it does pose questions from a feminist perspective: if the only jobs available will be in science and technology, how is that going to work for women in the light of the gender gaps in those professions? If we followed that route, would we be paving the way to men at work and women at home?

What we need is a progressive, enlightened digital politics aimed at getting the most out of technology: a better environment, better healthcare, a better work-life balance. To achieve that, we need better governance of AI – and women must be at the heart of this.

The Fabian Women's Network has decided it is time to take action and throw our weight behind the cause. In May 2018 we launched our Women Leading in AI series. At our first gathering we brought together some of the most interesting and thought-provoking female voices on AI, ranging from business and academia to think tanks. It is time for women not only to investigate what AI means for us, but also to make sure we frame and lead the debate about its governance and purpose, so it becomes a force for the common good and not the ultimate expression of masculine control.

(This article was first published in The Guardian on 13 March 2018.)

Some start fires

M W Bewick

For the world's hot air is waste, effluent,
and it dries voices to an earnest hush,
a warning that something approaches, quick
as a boomerang, fathomless but clear,
the return of some hard horror of which
we remain only casually aware.

The top man at the office lifts a hand,
fills his glass at the water cooler, casts
away profit warnings, checks his mirror,
mutters something about resilience,
while the heat chokes up his vacant city
until it can hardly breathe.
                                    This, already.

This silence – our silence – is what we hear,
a mouthed howl of loss, already knowing
the shouts in the street are gone, no witnesses
left in the empty parks, for those who can

are jailed indoors playing waiting games
with the nights of fever-pitched sleep to come.

To be cool, to be cooled, is to be rich.
The otherfolk slowly tread the concrete
while a hospital's heat wards fill with the poor,
the aged, the sick, the overweight, the frail,
and the victims of the surge in urban crime
trapped by the toxic city,

                      city of fire.

Temperatures hit 50 by dead degrees.
In Australia, the bush fires start in winter,
edge towards the cities of New South Wales
where swimming pools offer safety for cash.
Afternoon work becomes an outlawed pursuit
in Kuwait, where they've started harvesting fog.

The burning sky is deserted of birds,
asphalt melts under a Red-Listed lizard,
and your plastic office glass is flimsy
but corporate water is nice and cool.
Compromises will be made, and we must
escape from blaze after

                      blaze after blaze.

Some people start those fires, is what they say.
And oh, they really do, they really do.

Temple for Mithras

M W Bewick

City of light, concrete and colour
built from the strands of imperial dreams,
where are you to take me next?
Your embankments of sludge lined with planes,
bark and pollen strewn across markets,
across the dust of ancient temples,
blasting the paving from venal memory.
What flags hang from those baroque ideals?
Why are the flags waving now?
We are part of a journey, left to find
a city in amber, neither going nor coming,
exhibited in glass greased by palms.
The city as mosaic, city as relic.
The saints and artists scattered on the wind.
The barges on the tide, loaded with landfill
trash pushed anywhere out of sight.
Across a faded map of old lagoons,
floating people with thin ribs,
choking in lorries, detained and dying
in the heat of bureaucracy, the river slowed

to a standstill where boats brought spices and tea,
silver and slaves – and what that means
for us today: a bacchanalia for the few.
The spark of Mithras almost extinguished.
The shout of the street catching in my throat.

This is Earth

Wersha Bharadwa

'Listen darling, it's time for us to have the talk.'

My mother's face is pained.

I know what the talk is.

It's about rape.

They've being doing this on planet Earth for millennia. Humans invented a system called patriarchy around the Neolithic Era. In order to promote efficiency back during the trial period, they used various sugar-coated euphemisms such as 'seizing', or 'laying down,' and 'pursuing shared feelings' to diminish the brutality of rape. Next, the males reasoned patriarchy seemed like a good deal and gradually began to roll out the programme. One society at a time.

My mother's prepping me for my rite of passage: how to conduct myself in public, specifically in areas where men might be present.

'You got everything, honey?'

'Uh huh.'

'Because there's no room for interpretation,' my mother says. 'Anything above the ankle, and you can depend on human lawyers hanging you out to dry.'

'Like, how?'

'They go around saying you "advertised it".'

'Advertised what?'

'Your body. And its availability for being raped.'

I wink at her and point my finger in the air.

'Ha! But rape isn't only about sex! It's also about power, entitlement and revenge!'

My mother beams with pride and laughs.

We can make jokes like this on planet Zerg where it's safe to point out human stupidity and hypocrisy. Every male and female here is equal.

On Earth they have a long way to go.

They've even had to construct a word for the need to treat males and females equally: Feminism. It's pretty messed up down there.

My mother estimates it will take approximately 7,000 years for women to see some improvement. She bases this on her discovery that the term 'rape culture' was first being used by feminists in the 1970s but only became significant after a group of women in Toronto organised 'Slutwalks' in 2011. The females were protesting against a police officer who'd advised women at a university safety talk not to dress like sluts. A year later, the term was used again when a gang of men in Delhi raped and murdered a 12 year old girl called Jhoti Singh on a bus.

I thought the climate around rape and sexual assault had heated up so much by 2018 (triggered by a Hollywood producer and an American president) that everything would naturally cool down and male Earthlings would finally stop their raping. Turns out because they don't educate and hire an equal number of females in their world councils, businesses and governments, nothing changes.

We just don't have rape on Zerg. We're built and socially conditioned to identify with our female and male sides. Everyone's paid equal amounts for equal work and male Zergians don't need to be pumped for taking paternity leave, changing nappies or cooking for their wives. A lot of highly academic gap-year Zergians visit Earth to study the primitive systems of humanity. They do this by assuming human form. However, it's not the easy feat it once was – mainly because humans are already assuming other life forms by plumping their lips and cheeks with a substance called hyaluronic acid. Or they're having ops to shrink their noses.

Last week, my parents discovered Earthlings have been using artificial intelligence to help humans into space, most likely to colonise planets like Mars.

My mother, as one of the heads of the 10 Galaxies, simply decided enough is enough. She sent an email to every inhabitant of the 10 Galaxies two days ago:

From: Mehma Moja

To: (list) Inhabitants of the 10 Galaxies

Dear All,

As events on Earth continue to spiral out of control, it is time to be clear. For thousands of years humans have been given every opportunity to fix this, but refuse to enforce what is the key to peaceful living – equality. Unless they end the silencing and systematic persecution of females within seven days, the Council has decided to begin a permanent blockade of Earth. We cannot risk our peace or lives by allowing a cancerous ruling system – patriarchy – to infect our beloved planets. While the Council's decision is final, we will stand by the sacred Treaty of the 10 Galaxies. In accordance with our founding principle: 'Compassion

First', Earth will be sent a last-chance rescue worker tomorrow. The rescue worker will make every effort to ensure humans understand they can avoid their ultimate fate – most likely plastic contamination – if they meet next Friday's deadline. Thank you all for your cooperation.

For further information please contact the press office.

I'm the rescue worker.

'Sending her only child to Earth?!' Charlie, my best friend is screaming into the phone. 'Yo, we know what happens when we get involved in human shit!'

'You know why!' I snap. 'It's an important mission.'

'Yeah, but we learned in school how penetrating the Earth's atmosphere plays havoc with our genetic system! You ain't gonna be able to just pick up where you left off!'

It's a different ball game: choosing not to have kids is one thing, but no one likes being told they can't have them. Going to Earth means you age 500 Zerg years. The process is a bye-bye kiss to your biological clock. (That's why Zergs who take gap years on Earth are mostly dusty old academics).

The oldies have in-jokes about a foolproof birth control method: watching Earth's snowballing population and witnessing the failure of its religious-based abstinence programmes.

'Just remember,' Charlie says to me. 'Jesus. Joan of Arc! You know what happens to rescue-workers!'

'You forget, I'm infertile. I'm the perfect candidate for the mission.'

'You get home and the only guys left are the over 500s. Those guys have baggage—'

'Listen, I need to pack—'

'Neela, wait!'

Charlie's right, it does sound like the Jesus story. But here's the twist: I won't be sacrificing jack for humanity.

I've got a much better plan.

Later that day, my mother's making lava tea.

'Ma, I'm already wearing a burqa.'

'Contrary to popular human belief, burqas don't faze rapists,' she says. 'Look up ISIS and the use of mass rape as a weapon of war.'

'I know how to keep safe.'

'You don't get it,' she says. 'What you do doesn't matter. If you go out in public as a female, that's provocative. You must go stealth mode, darling.'

During my studies, I read how, in the 1980s, police and governments on Earth ran anti-rape campaigns warning women not to go out at night. They also gave tips on how to avoid being raped, like never leaving drinks unattended.

I wondered why the campaigns weren't aimed at preventing men from committing rape and reminding them they'd be jailed and put on life-long registers the way Zerg did when our first laws were first drafted?

'How will I get anything done by making myself invisible?'

'I'd prefer you not to do this mission at all.' My mother's voice breaks.

It takes a few Zerg light years zooming through space before I land on a children's playground. This is in a city called Birmingham in

England which is very popular among Zergs for Indian street food and snacks (which we all love).

'Go to Junaghar Sweet Centre, nowhere else,' my mother advised. 'Ask for a guy called Nikhil – he's the best.'

I don't have to ask for Nikhil because I can see he has a large tattoo of his name across his forearm. I briefly wonder if all humans do this and if forgetting who they are is a recurring problem.

'How can I help?' Nikhil asks. I end up ordering a plate of pani puri to eat in. He brings it over and starts talking so fast I just nod and smile. When I realise that we'll be talking a while, I move the chair next to me so he can sit.

I don't catch much except he's studying chemistry at Aston University and helps his parents run their shop. All this while I'm chomping and he's blathering on. And then I do my trademark act of telling guys every little thing about me, except this time I go into huge detail about my mission to Earth. I wait for him to interrupt me the way Charlie warned Earth men do whenever a female is speaking, or for him to call me crazy, but he doesn't. He has softly joined up eyebrows and crinkles under his eyes.

I figure it's going to be a lonely mission and even Jesus and Joan of Arc had a few buddies and so I ask Nikhil to join me.

'Slight problem: I can't fly at the speed of lightning,' he says.

'But you want to come, right?'

'It's just... my 'rents.'

'They won't let you?'

He struggles to speak.

'They're not prejudiced against me hanging out with aliens per se, they just want me to get married to an Indian Gujarati girl this year. Only son and all. My dad's made me pinky promise to God. I have back-to-back dates lined up all this week.'

'But you know there's no God, right?'

'I do now.'

'So come help me! Rearrange your dates for next week.'

'Okay, I'll message my mum.'

Nikhil seems like a good supporter and not at all like a rapist.

Yet even as I think the thought, alarm bells go off in my head. Is he?

I'd read Earth rapists are mostly guys you know and unless they're registered, there's no way you can identify one.

Being with Nikhil has been an education. Over the course of five days he's proved a hardworking and loyal partner. Zergians and all the 10 Galaxies are wrong about male Earthlings – they're not all the same. Other guys like Nikhil have been happy to help too. Nikhil's taught me that the patriarchy is nothing to do with being male.

Recruiting women to help save the planet has been easy. Historically, they've been ignored whenever they've spoken out, so they're empathetic to my mission. But it dawns on me I can't just use women to end the problems of patriarchy. We need more males on board to challenge the system.

Nikhil sorts out a way for us to teach male students about equality in schools. He is allowed to attend their assemblies and is a natural speaker. I wonder if the Gujarati girl he ends up marrying will think the same. When Nikhil holds the boys' attention by teaching them 'not to be rape apologists' and how 'just being a nice guy to other people doesn't mean he didn't rape her', I find my insides tingling. I give him a hug and he kisses me on the cheek.

'Rape isn't accidental,' Nikhil says in another packed school hall. 'From now on we only identify the root cause of rape: rapists.'

But it's not enough. Five days in and our message isn't making the global impact it needs to. It's not making much of an impact in Birmingham either. We need a better solution. Suddenly I have an epiphany. This must be how human females feel while hurdling all the obstacles life puts in their way. How they manage to smile or use lipstick is beyond me.

We have no choice but to infiltrate the next world leaders' meeting. Luckily, Earth has a similar event to our 10 Galaxies Council AGM – it's called the G8 Summit.

'Why are we at Gleneagles?' Nikhil has his glasses on. He's super cute in them.

I tell him the G8 Summit sounds like a good place to reason with Earth's leaders. How these are the most powerful men and women in the world and if I can just convince them of why patriarchy is already hurting them, I might not have to disclose how they've no time before they're all consigned to their doom.

'How did you get in, Miss...?'

'Neela. And this is Nikhil.'

I use telekinesis to lock the doors from the inside. How do you calm down a group of angry, frightened presidents and prime ministers?

'Someone call security now!'

'No! Honestly you don't have to! We come in peace.'

Nikhil motions to me and whispers. 'That's what all aliens say. You've got to be more original.'

I rush to the room's main computer system, stick my USB in and load up the powerpoint presentation I wrote earlier onto the viewer.

Everybody's staring at me. It's exactly like the time I won the Galaxy DJ competition, except not in a nice way. One man in a suit is holding his hand over his chest – a signal I've read humans use to tell you they're about to go into cardiac arrest.

'I'll give it to you straight: You have exactly one day to sort out Earth's raping and gender equality crisis before the leaders of Zerg, my home planet, and the 10 Galaxies block humans from travelling into space. That means no Mars missions and certain death from the plastic waste and overheating problems you guys have caused.'

'Security!'

'When societies educate all women it leads to greater economic output—'

'She's a radical! Ahhhhhh!!!'

'Hear me out! Just look at Iceland—'

'Does anyone in this room have a gun?!'

Nikhil grabs me and we rush down the emergency exit stairs back to my car. We get shot at and chased for a couple of minutes before I'm able to buckle my seat-belt and command the vehicle to go back to invisible mode.

'Why didn't you just listen to me?' Nikhil's upset. I avert my eyes and keep driving through the Scottish highlands. It's pretty around here.

'You nearly got us killed!'

'Those guys in that room? Your 'world leaders?' Are they all like that?'

'Kind of!'

'Even the females?'

'I guess so! And they're all into capitalism, which if you'd asked me – is the bigger overall problem on Earth. Or maybe it's a bad combi deal of capitalism and patriarchy.'

'Whatever it is, it's over. You guys are toast.'

I cry. Nikhil puts one hand to my cheek and wipes away my

tears with the other. I stop the car and we share a kiss. I feel homesick but also realise I am in love.

From: Neela Moja

To: Mehma Moja

Dear Mama,

I am sad to say the mission has failed. The humans captured me last night. Sadly I'm now awaiting execution as a witch. Yes, mother, Earth's politicians have used my campaign to save them to pass legislation sanctioning the burning of witches again. Earth has regressed to the 1600s, all because of me. I've already been beaten bloody, dragged through the streets and spat at.

My feet are shackled but they were cool about letting me use my tablet for sending emails. Two prison guards talked about raping me this morning but then decided against it because I reminded them I was a witch and forced entry would cause their penises to rot off. They didn't fancy their chances.

Obviously, I can't die the human way, but they've found a way to torture the living daylights out of me. I've never felt such white hot pain in my life. They will 'kill' me by tying my feet to a lead weight and throwing me in the sea. Of course I can breathe underwater, free myself and get home, but they don't know that. Being more of a 'run-on-the-beach' rather than a 'swim-in-the-ocean' type, I'm not looking forward to the next few hours. However I'll be home soon, mission failed.

PS I've also fallen for Nikhil. He's in the cell next to me. They'll burn him alive under the new witchcraft laws. I can't save him. It sucks.

'How did it go?' Charlie's instant messaging me.

'All the humans on Earth were destroyed – well the ones who refused to accept equality. Didn't you hear?'

'Someone mentioned it over dinner – I'm still on my silent retreat.'

'How's it going?'

'Great, except I want to mainline instant messenger. We're not allowed phones, laptops or telekinesis. But there's a lot of sex going on.'

'Really? I'm on every news channel.'

'How come they got so drastic?'

'So my Mum came down just as I was about to be 'drowned' and announced the original plan was to blockade their entry into space but what would I like to do in light of recent events? So I realised, actually while the blockade solved the problem for the 10 Galaxies, it didn't solve the problem for good humans like Nikhil. So I asked mum to deliver a killer virus to all the toxic assholes while rescuing all the good guys, animals and plants. We've enough room on Zerg and the other planets. She agreed.'

'Oh wow – congratulations! Have you got it together with Nikhil?'

'No. But I've found him a place to live while Mum helps him get a job.'

The rescued humans are integrating brilliantly. The days of women needing to be on sober rape watch are gone. They no longer live in fear of being jailed for hitting out at their attackers in self-defence, or of ex-boyfriend's plastering compromising photos of them on the internet. Everybody's safe and happy. The people who remember Earth's old ways have readily discarded those systems. I think a big deterrent was also seeing their colleagues, neighbours, friends and families being attacked by a stonking killer disease. Female Earthlings enjoy access to jobs and education and have full control over their reproductive rights. Back on Earth, the planet is essentially healing itself. The rainforests are growing back once more.

Nikhil has asked me to marry him. I've said yes.

The cowboy with the calcium spur

Mark Brayley

The mother, proud but post-natal, tired and torn,
sat at the side of the white jailhouse cowboy cot
and sighed a stifled smile for her infant newborn.
The father was out, celebrating his white hot

virility with good scotch and better wishes.
Alone, at home, the new mother was not to know
that simple fear for the future diminishes
us all. How, in time, will her newborn baby grow?

Will he be a cowboy with a calcium spur,
brittle, SANE, fit for office, and medically
exempt from the poor's selective service, yes sir,
but, no, not exempt from golf? Momentarily,

the mother looks at the book, *Baby and Child Care.*
Despite her well-stuck fears, she knows that she knows best
and the justification will be found right there
on page sixty-eight. Spock spoke for the dispossessed

one hundred, two hundred or five hundred thousand.
With no force, and no violence but otherwise
the permissive men and women across the land
proved just too pampered to permit their own demise.

Eclipse

Catherine Coldstream

And take him with you, they said,
cold as paper and ink, a
contract.

Lines eked from the
pen, tract in the snow,
unaccountable pale traction.

It shouldn't feel like this, we said.
Lonely faces, eclipsed behind clear glass,
Invisible attraction.

Take him with you,
They said.
No retraction.

Futile to recourse to action, so
we slung our stones into
rucksacks warm in the act of
walking in bare sunlight
and the loaves we'd baked
earlier, in the cottage where we'd
slept too long.

Into the bluebell wood
we went and remembered
what we'd been told at the outset:
take your ticket. Friction.
No reaction.

American beauty

Guy de Cruz

Magazine shoes and magazine hair
and magazine looks and magazine stare
and magazine hot from emptied clip
temple hole red matches magazine lips.
And magazine rouge on bloodied cheek
and magazine entry all quiet and sleek adds
red upon red to magazine face all twisted
and gurning with slaughterhouse taste.
And heroin chic from magazine page
unimportant in the face of
face off from magazine rage.
And size zero try smaller
and smaller and rot down
and magazine columns and magazine lines
and magazine steel prompts wondering minds
and magazine headlines and magazine news
and American beauty
gunned out of its shoe.

The walking stick

Peter Fullagar

It hadn't been that long since it had happened. The decision had been made, the democratic process at its worst. All those months of negotiating, meetings, proposals. And for what? For this? Is this what we have ended up with?

I watch as the discarded crisp packet swiftly cartwheels past my foot, shine that has lost its fervour; mattified into a faded vision of the past; less a symbol than an effigy of our throwaway society. Freewheeling, the packet continues until it comes to rest against a wall of black bags, flicked cigarette butts and soiled nappies. What was it that Madonna sang? *This used to be my playground.*

My back prickles from the heat of my body against the brick wall. It itches. Turning away from the ever-growing mountain of rubbish, I notice another 'For Sale' sign across the street. From where I sit, I now count them. Seven, and that's just in my line of sight. This was a thriving community until...

Lights burning through curtains, hunting for car space and the noise. The noise was wonderful. It sounded like a playground. I remember when Ágnes slipped off the kerb and grazed her knee; the noise that girl could make was striking. I forget her mother's name, but she rushed out of her house to comfort the child. She swept Ági up into her arms and disappeared into the house to the clamour of voices. Three weeks ago now? The sign went up around then. Such a nice family; I miss them.

Glancing at my watch and sighing, I need to stand up and walk away from the trash mountain – in the heat, the stench is unbearable. I walk down the street towards West Road. I frantically check my pockets for my blue book. Yes, in the back-left pocket of my ripped jeans; that little blue book is my ticket. My ticket to brighter days and a richer future. Burning a hole in my pocket, it almost glows with intense pride.

Reaching the junction, I stop and look. To the left is another pile of bags, filled with detritus of happier times. Prosperous times. Ironic that the rubbish has returned to its origin of sale. The bags reliant on boarded-up windows. The paper shop is what we used to call it: penny sweets, disinfectant and incense sticks. That waft of frankincense emanating from the door, every time it was pushed open. It was always frankincense. If I break the lock, or smash the window in, I'll get that scent again. It's almost worth it to be enveloped in those days again.

Not wanting to lose the power of my blue book, I decide to turn right. There was a café in this direction, and I need some coffee.

The desolation on West Road is evident. The surgery stands naked, with shards of glass pointing skywards where the window once was. There hasn't been a doctor here for weeks, let alone patients. Now if I need a shot, I have to go to the Centralised Zone and see Dr Brown. She's good, but I imagine she's soon to retire. The old station sits opposite, but the shutters were closed months ago. The lines only run to the edges of the CZ. The lines inside are well maintained and run on time, but travel outside of the Zone, and it's either walk or wait for a bus. I can't look at the station for long; too many memories. Slava. My friend. He worked in the ticket office for years and he was the soul of the station with his hearty chants and dreadful jokes that even he didn't understand – but he was the highlight of my morning commute as I'm sure he was for others.

Mario's café on the corner is a hive of activity as usual. A throng of kids huddled by the window greedily slurp their coffees. The girls cling onto the boys as if marking their territory. Stains of coffee litter the pavement, spreading from the wide, friendly door. Checking my wallet in my left pocket, I step into the café and pass by small, individual colonies of people, deep in their own conversations, seated around circular tables with red and white striped plastic tablecloths. Sidestepping a couple of crowded tables, I make my way to the main counter and stand behind a young lady and an older gentleman who is leaning on a walking stick. They're not together, I think – both of them stare straight ahead at the barista next to the coffee machine. This pair don't interest me, but the stick is fascinating; gnarled and knobbly, it has never been straight. Oak, perhaps. Clasped in the equally gnarled hand sparkles of silver; a shimmering eagle's head, sitting proudly atop the wood. I wonder about the origins of the stick and how it came to be propping up this old man up in the café. Suddenly, the eagle drops towards the floor and I watch it twist and flail in slow motion until it meets the tiles with a sharp shock. Carefully lifting the head off the floor, I return the stick to the man with a smile, and receive a grin in return. But it is then I notice his eyes; dark hazel with a shining glint that speaks to me and prompts me to recollect past times. Mournful longing for a bygone age. I feel it too. *Those were the days.* Mary Hopkin. Bewitched by the tune, I hardly notice the man limp past me, clutching his coffee. The young lady is long gone. Back to the present, I make murmurings of small talk with Manuel the barista while I wait for my drink. Manuel still can't believe he has Special Dispensation. I hear this every time and it's tiresome. I take my coffee and head for the door, trying to avoid the clattering groups at the tables, finally passing into the open to take a quick, but scalding, sip of coffee.

I'm almost at the CZ now – the giant glass structures are impossible to miss. Imposing and fully automated, I see no reason for the guards stationed behind the glass. There must be at least twenty of these gates around the edge of the CZ, all automated yet still guarded. As I approach my gate, I reach into my back-left pocket and pull the blue book into view and slam it onto the scanner. A second later, the automaton beeps, the doors slide open to let me in and I step through.

The Weathermaton programme for the day is to be 20 degrees and sunny, with a light, but pleasant, south-easterly breeze. My shadow stretches behind me as I walk towards the station. I hop onto the train that's already waiting and the doors close. I stand in my usual spot, staring out of the window to the north and remind myself that nothing ever seems to change within the CZ. Except that everything has changed. Irrevocably. The trees that line the streets below me are the same. The office blocks and skyscrapers; the trampolines in every rear garden; crumbling roof tiles; the same. Twitching curtains behind smeared windows; the same. Occupants doing the twitching; replaced. Well, half of them anyway. The blue book? Entrance ticket to the CZ.

The train slows to my stop, and I leave my now-empty cup on the floor. Only a handful of commuters leave with me, and we exit the station into the wide and glaring scene of the Square. The expanse is enormous, like Red Square on steroids. The Square is busy for a Tuesday morning. Black bowlers and umbrellas bob along as the owners attempt to reach their destinations. Power suits and high heels clamour for every cobbled inch, darting west to east, north to south, heads down, saying nothing. The stalls lining the perimeter of the Square are drumming up their everyday business; sandwiches, hot soup and tea – the staples of the CZ. I grab a cheddar bap but yearn for the succulent taste of Gouda. Not much choice nowadays; cheddar or Wensleydale and that's about it. My lunch eaten, I head to the school.

School number 47, five minutes north west of the Square, are towers like a beacon of future hope, concealing a former embassy with languages echoing round the corridors. I reach again for the blue book and scan my way into the building. Being a First National Educator, I have the power to demand evidence of the pupils' blue book status – the Premier NE encourages it, although we FNEs skip this order most of the time. Passing through the hallways, I come to my room on the ground floor and enter. I check the blue books sitting on the right corner of each of the fifty desks, which eats into the lesson time. Today, the topic is language – English, naturally, and we continue, looking at adjectival phrases and enhancing the beauty of the language.

Seven periods later, we're chanting the Anthem, signifying the end of the learning day – the pupils disperse, leaving the school to join the race to their homes. They're lucky if they reside within the CZ – all the benefits of the change with none of the dirt and chaos that lies outside. I follow them at a slower pace, passing uncomfortably into the afternoon rush. Is this all there is? The better and brighter future? We gained control of ourselves, yet we didn't even know how to govern properly. We wanted something different, but we didn't know what that would mean. And now here we are; segregated, isolated and agitated. This isn't what I wanted, not at all. The fury starts to rise up inside my body until my fingers begin to shake. Keeping my head low, I thrust my hands deep into my pockets trying not to be noticed. The Square is half as crowded now so it's simple to traverse the cobbles towards the station. The daily protestors standing outside with their placards voicing support for purity, singularity and nationalism. Their blue uniforms lose their impact in the fading light. I cower further into myself as I speed past their signs and into the station. The recorded announcement states that the doors will close imminently, before the train heads off in the direction of the Western Gate. Once more, the train moves silently off, and I stare to the south. The communities have lost their diversity, the thrill of difference. I focus on the church spire in the distance. Silhouetted, the cross appears to be straining upwards, reaching as high as it can to escape the new, every day normality. Flickering lights at the windows indicate a presence within. I squint to imagine, to remember, what it was like before. I drift into a sense of bliss, remembering the imperfections, but I'm interrupted by the train slowing for the final stop.

Exiting the train, my mind is exhausted and the exhaustion diffuses into my body; I can't help but slump against the wall outside the station. My head comes to rest in my hands as I bring my knees up while the workers make a beeline for the scanning gate to leave the CZ. When did we become this way? Where is our openness? I slowly lift my head to survey the scene unfolding before me. The stunning glass towers, standing tall, unmovable, lose their shine at the closure of the day. The guards, faceless, emotionless, are still stationed in their place by the scanner, but safely on this side of the zone.

To the side of the scanners, I notice something softly glinting in the lights of the guard office, propped against the wall. Hauling myself to my feet, I walk directly towards the office. Ensuring I don't trip over the workers, I crisscross the advancing line, closing in on the office. Within ten metres, I recognise the item – the walking stick with the eagle head. Touching distance now, I see that it's a different stick, but still with a bird's head – this time, it's a swallow, shining in gold. I'm reminded of the old man and his eyes. Those dark, hazel eyes. A wave of emotion comes over me as I run my shaking fingers over the head. Clasping my hand around the skull, I lift the stick from its prone position, and it suddenly comes alive. The power is forceful, and before I know it, I'm walking away, still holding the stick. It feels good; comfortable. I feel... changed. I see it all now. This needs to happen. The CZ, The FNEs; they need to change.

The blue book remains firmly out of sight as I head towards the glass container that we've put ourselves in. I raise the stick, and with all the fight left in me, I thrust the swallow's head at the glass that separates us. The guards glance my way but do nothing – a small crack appears. I repeat the motion, hurling the swallow at the crack, and it gets bigger, and by now, I'm shouting and shrieking at the inequality we have encased ourselves in. The crack multiplies, and reaches further from the epicentre, searching for more weaknesses in the structure. Again and again, the swallow crashes against the glass until eventually the head creates a small hole and the stick crumbles and breaks. I drop the broken tool, and use my fists to smash through the glass, shattering the wall which rains down on my head until drops of blood start to blur my vision. The wall is broken and I step through the opening to the familiar scent of frankincense. That sweet smell of the before and I realise that all it took to break the new world was me.

Save me from the dogs

J L Hall

He is here. Crossing the bulevard from the Gara de Nord. A lavender dusk falls over Bucureşti as he weaves between the cars, his wristwatch glints in the streetlights. He is coming to meet me again, we must always be unseen. I stand in the shadows, with my back pressed to trunk of our tree, I dip my head. He takes my hand, 'draga Raluca,' he says. I freeze, certain that I hear the whir of the CCTV as it turns its camera towards us, to find my face. They watch all day and all night for us, we who must live in the underworld. I can hear a dog barking, somewhere.

I was high on aurolac, giddy and febrile, when I first met Constantin. My young brother Andru and I had stolen up onto Bulevardul Dinicu Golescu to buy some cola and firewater. Our mission was to rob tourists at the train station; their phones, their wristwatches and wallets, any small bags. We have no money ourselves, we copiii strazii, street-children. Andru had brought his blade to the ribs of a tourist and we were running back before the cameras caught us, when I stopped. Constantin. My breath left me, and the world stilled: his suit, his mouth, the coil of nicotine from his lips. His eyes on mine. He was so close I could almost touch him. He smiled and began to speak. 'Luca,' Andru yelled, frowning at Constantin, and scraped the manhole cover back. He disappeared down the hole, tugging my ankle to follow. A siren. A dog. I slipped beneath the surface and out of sight.

I remember the first time Constantin and I took the taxi together in July. It was twenty-eight degrees outside and I could feel the heat from him, and the warmth from the car's engine under my thighs. I could smell myself, the aurolac leaching from my pores, and odour from my armpits and crotch, so I wound down the window and breathed in the hot night air. When we reached his apartment, he let me shower, he fed me: some 'antipasti,' he called it; salami and cheeses, and mamaliga, a polenta with garlic sauce. 'I want to look after you,' he said. He murmured it later into my nape, my hair scented with mint and eucalyptus from his shower-gel. I believed him straight away, sated with food and love. Constantin was a man who could protect me, who could save me. He drove me back to Andru when everyone was still unconscious or too high to notice. It was the first time I had ever left my brother since he was born, and guilt slicked my skin like oil.

Tonight Andru and I drop again beneath the bulevard. We pass through air clouded silver with aurolac and deafening techno and suffocating heat as I crawl along the sewer tunnel after my brother. He swaggers across the chamber to King, handing him the wallets and wristwatches, the cola and firewater. King ruffles his hair, before punching Andru lightly on the arm and handing him his plastic bag of aurolac. Andru doesn't like it when you treat him like a child. At fourteen, and three years younger than me, he is small for his age, his voice not yet broken. He has inhaled too much, like the rest of us. He idolises King, the only father he has ever known. He mimics him: his topknot, his strut, his man's cough, his stolen chains and jewels. I think Andru almost wishes for the dog bites that King has on his calves and forearms, that he has tattooed around with Orthodox crosses, bites from the times they almost caught him but, he said, God saved him.

Later, I lie on my bunk and twist to face the wall. The bunk creaks and groans like the sound of a last breath. I smooth my hand over the wall, smearing the dirt and condensation, moulding my fingertips to its crevices. I imagine Constantin's cotton sheets, and I trace a heart. I can feel his kiss on the cup of my palm as he said: 'tomorrow night, then, at our tree, you and Andru. 2.00 a.m. Be ready.'

'Stop moving,' Andru slurs from beneath me. 'Sleep!'

I smile. Tomorrow we will be a family: Constantin, Andru and me.

I wake around midday to see King counting out some stolen lei on the bunk that was Katarina's bed, in the corner of the room by my feet. She has been dead around ten weeks now, ripped to shreds by the dogs when she tried to escape from here. If the dogs hadn't caught her, AIDS would have killed her; her arms, legs, then groin were punctured with needle-pricks, and she was becoming really ill. She used to whisper to me at night, propped up on her elbows, her collar-bone jutting and eye-sockets hollow, that King would see her dead. 'He will never let us leave,' she mouthed. Katarina had almost made it to the tram stop at Piata Victoriei that night, and had lain in a tarry pool of blood in the middle of the bulevard. Later, after we had mourned and packed away our shrine, King said that she had died because their software recognised her face from their database; that's why they send the dogs. They modify their genes and breed them specifically to kill. He held a finger aloft, pointing towards the CCTV camera far above us, above the street in the sky, always watching, ready to hunt us down.

With Katarina gone, I am the eldest after King, then Irina, Samson, Macarena, Tudor, Maria, Viorel, Vasile, and Daciana. King has rescued all us copiii strazii, giving us shelter, food, drugs, and a twisted kinship that we cannot escape from. King trusts me to help him run our home; he thinks this binds me to him, this glue of duty and fear, but he is wrong.

King finishes counting and rolls up the notes, tying them with a spare hair band, before locking them in the safe. He wears the key around his wrist, another charm on his bracelet. He nudges my ankle, and nods toward the kitchen. The others are rousing from sleep and are hungry, my job every day is breakfast. As I sit up and peer below me to check that Andru is still sleeping, I feel King watching me from the corner of his eye, studying me as if to see what is different. I try to appear as haggard as possible, a frown, a slump in my shoulders. I make a show of rubbing the slumber and the aurolac from my eyes. I cough, and agree to his command in a newly hoarse voice.

I sniff the eggs to check that they are still fresh, the UHT milk is fine. Our fridge has been unreliable for the last few weeks or so, petering out at times. King had said the other day that they are trying to isolate the electricity to the sewers to flush us out. Daciana, at eight, the youngest of us, began to cry at this. 'What if they fix the manhole so that we can't get out? We would die!' King scooped her in his arms and held her, soothed her; she is his favourite. He was quick to reassure us all then, his voice boomed: 'They want to keep us off the streets, they don't want us dead, just invisible. Remember that.' He grew louder, shouting above the music, across the clouds of aurolac smoke. 'They can't kill us all at once, other countries wouldn't stand for it.' He stared at me; it was my cue to confirm this. I forced a smile for Daciana and Andru, doubting, as I do with most of what King says, that it was the truth.

I beat the eggs with a little milk in a bowl and dip slices of bread into it. French Toast is our staple breakfast: with cheap white bread it goes far, there are eleven of us to feed now Katarina is dead. As I drop the bread into the frying pan, it spits, and I jump back. King is behind me. 'You and Andru did good last night,' he says. 'We have enough lei to feed us all for three, four days, but we need more.' He stares at me for a long time, a puzzle he is trying to solve where the pieces no longer fit together. He doesn't move his eyes from me as he speaks. 'We can't risk you being seen tonight. I'll send Irina and Samson instead.' My heart sinks. I panic. I open my mouth to protest, even to plead that it is good for Andru to get some air, to clear his lungs, but he silences me with a look. He points towards the pan. 'It's sticking, you need to turn it.' He lays a hand on my shoulder for a little too long, and grips a little too hard. I resist the urge to pull away, I know better.

Later, when most of us are drugged or dozing, I squeeze onto Andru's bunk. He whines that I am taking up room. I lie down beside him, and loop my arm around his bony ribs. He is still small enough to fit under my chin; I rub my jaw from side to side across his crown and he slaps my arm. I laugh. He has always hated this, even in Orphanage 9 when we only had each other, he would wriggle out from under me.

I lay with him like this the night before the nurse helped us escape from the orphanage. She promised to bring us to a family who wanted us, who lived in a large house with a garden where we would have a bedroom each in Primaverii, a wealthy Bucureşti suburb. She lied, taking the couple's money and dumping us at Piata Victoriei amongst other copiii strazii, where, days later and starving and frightened, King gave us shelter. This was five years ago, Andru was so young and he clung to me for weeks. Leaving again will terrify him now, but his staying behind is not an option.

I tickle him, 'Andru,' I tease. He slaps me again, and begins to struggle away, but I hold him fast, gripping his wrists. My voice cracks as I whisper in his ear. 'What if we could leave here, just you and me?' He stiffens, and begins to turn towards me; I can feel him holding his breath. I smooth his hair from his forehead. I tell him everything.

In the afternoon, I watch from my bunk as Andru listens to King. King is showing him and Vasile how to repair an old laptop that he had found, he said, inside an old beat-up Audi down towards Piata Victoriei. He is explaining to them that the processor overheats, and so they need to fix the fan. My brother is small beside him, his narrow shoulders pressed in against King's elbow. They pore over the computer together; their voices are low beneath the music. The sinews in King's forearms are as thick as twine; his shifting bite scars and tattoos are a terrifying animation as he passes parts to Andru in his huge hands. This is Andru's favourite job. It passes the time while each day his life fades a little more.

King steps away to rummage in the drawer for a smaller screwdriver, glancing at me as he passes. Andru's eyes are large and high and they follow King devotedly back and forth. Andru hasn't looked at me since I told him about my plan to escape tonight. After I told him that I had been visiting Constantin every night, he fell silent and hasn't spoken to me since.

In the evening, while King and the others are laughing and drinking on the crates in the chamber, I steal a spare plastic bag from the drawer. I will fill it with a change of clothes for me and Andru later. Andru is avoiding me; every excuse I find to talk to him or pretence I make of asking for his help with something, he slips away from. He is drinking more than normal, sharing clouded bags of aurolac with Samson and King. I find a half-full bottle of cola and sip from it, wondering how to lure Andru away to talk.

At the far end of the chamber, I realise King is watching me. He ends his conversations with Tudor and Maria, and walks over to me. He holds out a hand. I pass him the cola, and watch him take a few mouthfuls.

'What's with you and Andru?' He grins.

I panic, unable to feign surprise or confusion. 'Nothing,' I blurt out.

'Nothing.' He repeats, his grin fading. Not for the first time his mood switches in an instant, his eyes flashing black; a warning.

He pokes my shoulder; his eyes are steely. 'You need to relax,' he says. 'Come,' he steps away and motions for me to follow. He sits on a crate and nods to the one beside him. He scoops some silver paint from a nearby tin into a bag and puffs into it. He passes it to me.

I wave a hand, 'No. I have a headache,' I lie.

He leans forward and cups my chin, placing the bag against my lips and lifting my hands to hold it. He watches me until I breathe, and breathe. I imagine dogs barking somewhere, and I picture Constantin's face until I cannot see anymore.

I wake with a start after 1.00 a.m., the base of the techno still pounds around the chamber. Silver mist hangs in veils between us. The smaller children are asleep, the older kids injecting heroin or puffing in and out of bags. Despite the music there is a feeling of quiet, of catatonia. King is the last one conscious but he eventually groans and slumps back on his bunk, his lids closing. He rests a scarred hand inside the belt of his jeans, the other arm drops to the ground.

I slip from my bunk and sink to my knees on the floor; the room spins. 'Come on,' I whisper to Andru, and pull him upright on his bunk. I give his shoulders a rough shake.

'No,' he mutters.

'You can't say no,' I slur. I shake him again. He is almost passing out, his eyes tilting towards the ceiling. I slap his cheeks to rouse him. 'It's time. The only chance. You and me.'

'And Constantin,' he scowls.

'Yes, we'll be a family.' I start to tip-toe around our bunks. In slow, silent motion I fill the plastic bag with a t-shirt for him, some underwear. I roll the bag, squashing it down against my knees, and tuck it into my waistband. 'Come on!' I hiss.

'No.'

I squat down before him, checking that King is still unconscious when I speak. I point my finger to the ceiling. 'Outside is better, we will stay with Constantin and you will finish school. You can get a job, maybe fixing computers. You will have your own sofa-bed.' Andru winces, and I realise my nails are cutting into his wrists.

'You promised me when we came here that you would never leave me.' He will not turn to me, his face is broken, his head low.

There is a blade in my heart. This is a choice I cannot make.

I do not look at Andru as I ease the manhole cover above me to one side. He is sobbing and pulling at my calf, he is begging me: 'Don't go, please, don't leave us. You swore to me.' He is choking and retching. I make myself turn and take one last glance at him. I am unable to speak, I reach out my hand to clutch at him, to drag him with me against his will but he steps back, his face dissolving with hurt. 'I will come for you, I promise,' I whisper.

I pull myself up onto the tarmac. I stumble to my feet and run between cars and taxis, racing to the shadows on the other side. I press myself into our tree, only peering out from behind it each time a car slows. I inch forward and scan up and down the bulevard. I try to calm my pulse; my stomach lurches, I have to stop myself from being sick. The cooler fresh air is hitting me hard tonight, I am reeling from the extra aurolac.

The traffic lights switch from red to amber to green and the cars speed by. Still Constantin is not here. What if he lied? I swat at a mosquito buzzing around me when I realise that it isn't the insect's whine I hear, but the whir of the camera. In my panic, I stare upwards, realising too late, and then dart again behind the tree. I crouch down, I am shaking, I am going to vomit. I crawl on all fours to peek around the tree and that is when I see Constantin's car, slowing on the far side of the road preparing to do a U-turn to come here, to me, to rescue me. He flashes his headlights and raises his hand through the open window, his watch glints in the street light. He smiles.

I am crying now, relieved to the point of collapse. I stagger out from behind the tree and onto the pavement, and it is then that I hear the thunder and snarling of dogs, eight, maybe ten, as black as Satan and charging towards me.

I scream, and then I run.

Rage

Sam Jordison

I'm trying to remember the last time I went through twenty four hours without feeling angry. Not angry in the stubbed-my-toe sense, or in flailing at any of the other pinpricks of existence. But a steady, determined, simmering perma-rage that I sometimes briefly forget, or suppress, but which boils over at least once a day and often more. Especially if – and this happened just before I started writing this article – Nigel Farage's face appears on my computer screen. His shit-balloon face. Those diamond hard eyes pricked into that inflated pig-flesh. His...

... Sorry. I did say I was angry. Anyway, towards the beginning of 2018, I went to India, and think I may have had a day, maybe, on a train, away from social media, rattling through beautiful countryside and bustling cities, realising that there was a wider world. Understanding that life went on away from Daily Mail island, and that most sane people on the planet neither know nor care about most of the things that are tormenting me. They haven't even heard of the gnome-faced UK Labour Party leader Jeremy Corbyn, let alone his failure to oppose the government's disastrous Brexit policies. And if you tell them about Arron Banks's Russian connections you'd just elicit a blank shrug.

In India, I also got food poisoning and that briefly focused my attention away from the fact that a mob of lying racists had ruined my daughter's future. But, otherwise: jeesh. I've been living with a monster in my belly, a cold hand around my heart, a fire behind my eyeballs for far, far too long.

It's not healthy. I don't like it. I'm not proud of it. Objectively, I know that rage is one of the world's big problems. It is not a good way to solve anything. Practically, I know that looking at people on the streets and wondering which of them voted to take so many rights away from my European friends in the UK, which of them saw the racism of the Leave campaign and decided that was the side they wanted to be on, which of them knew so little about economics that...

... There you go. Rage again. Stops you thinking in straight lines. Makes you ranty. And prone to write in semi-articulate lists. But you should just be glad you're reading this essay rather than my Twitter stream around late June 2016. Which, of course, was when things got really bad. Even worse, I should say. I'd already been losing my shit for a while. Everyone knows the story, so I won't repeat it. And I'm guessing it's no fun for anyone reading this to be reminded of the run up to the June 2016 referendum, the horrible vertiginous feeling of falling away from our old certainties, and of seeing truth plummeting alongside us.

Ugh.

I'm writing this in June 2018, and it still feels like we're falling. Brexit hasn't yet happened, Trump isn't even half way through his first term. The floor is rising up to meet us, and I'm really not looking forward to impact. But the sense of spinning though the air, the helpless flailing. I could do without that too.

It makes me long for the days before we got pushed off the cliff edge. It might be my rose-tinted vision, but I'm sure there was a period in the late 1990s, before 9/11 and everything else, when the legalisation of weed felt like the most pressing political issue. Can you imagine? Weed! Who cares? But it was on the front page of my newspaper every Sunday. The very idea is as old-fashioned as actually reading a Sunday newspaper. Not the idea of legalisation. The idea of anyone caring. Now they're actually on the verge of allowing medical marijuana to be used in the UK it and no one gives a stuff. It makes me yearn for the days of pointless police oppression of stoners. You know, instead of actual fascism...

And okay. I know nostalgia isn't that healthy, either. One of my pet theories is that it was longing for a non-existent past that got us into this mess in the first place. I'm pretty sure a lot of the Leave Vote was inspired by misplaced yearning for the years when Baby-Boomer voters didn't have such bad backs, still had flowing locks and something more to look forward to than nights in watching repeats of Mrs Browns' Boys. They imagined that everything was better before we joined the EU, because that was when they personally felt better.

They were wrong, clearly. And look where they got us. But I can understand the appeal of that kind of thinking. I have a similarly glowing vision of my own late teens and twenties. It came a little later. But that time too feels like a far off and unattainable dream. A golden age when we weren't all arguing. We were mainly just trying to turn relaxing into an artform:

'What are you doing?'

'I'm chilling.'

'What's the bar like?'

'Pretty chilled.'

'Is Steve okay?'

'Yeah, he's chill.'

I'm slightly embarrassed that we used to talk like that. It's probably a reasonably strong argument against allowing people to consume soft drugs. Even so, I'm more sad that we don't work on our mellow any more. I miss it. It's so hard to think of anyone describing themselves as 'chilled' today:

'Oh yes, I'm chilled.'

'What the fuck is wrong with you? Wake up! Have you not looked out the window lately. Fucking everything is on fire!'

So: chilling. No longer a valid option. But as I say, I don't think getting angry is helping much either. Speaking personally, I don't think I've managed to do anything constructive to get us out of this hole. I've written irate books. I've got into pointless fights on social media. I've marched several times through London with people singing about Jeremy's Corbyn's failure to oppose, about how unwelcome Trump is in the UK, about Boris Johnson's lies.... And it's all felt cathartic. But what else? Where are we now? How have we progressed? What have I done, except contribute to the noise of it all, the endless buzzing and stinging, the wasp's nest in our communal attic...

And look at me now. I'm doing it again. Thumping out more words. More bile. And pretty much the only thing I've achieved in writing this essay is to convince myself of the pointlessness of it all. I wish I could give you a definite conclusion. I wish I could direct you somewhere useful. But in all honesty, this circular babble feels more true to our times. I'm spinning around eating my own tail. Like a crazy dog. Like everyone else.

Still, I guess I'd rather look at my own metaphorical rear end than think about Nigel Farage's face, as I was just before I started writing this piece. Perhaps there's something to be said for focusing on the anger, after all...

A tasty morsel

Emma Kittle-Pey

When you arrived home early that day, I said, 'I have to go and get compost and supplies.'

And you sighed your sigh. 'Why can't you get a proper job, like me, like Marjorie?'

When I left you inspected the kitchen, the calendar, and said, 'Oh, look, Olive. Has mummy *not* made a cake for the PTA bake? Typical eh?' Tap, tap. Tap, tap. Swipe.

'Don't worry,' said Olive, 'we can make one, let's make a cake for the PTA bake!' Climbing onto a chair, pulling the eggs from the fridge, dropping them onto the kitchen floor. Sticky whites seeped through the box, lips pursed, you plucked out the two whole eggs. You measured out half the flour, half the sugar and half the butter. Olive poured in the sea-salt as the phone bleeped. When you answered she spilt the milk over the counter.

While Storm Belinda slyly whipped the outgoing tide into a small frenzy, I, the Seaweed Collector, had waded a little too far around the bay, and was grabbing at the long weed on the rocks, trying to scramble up before I was thrown against them. Sliding down the rock face as the waves retreated, grasping at the strong kelp, picking the thick ribbons over the weak leaf-weed.

You noticed the froth at the milky shore-line, the white liquid polluted by lumps of brown sugar, Olive pushing it around, wrinkling her nose. Erupting inside, as the doorbell chimed, and thankfully there was Marjorie from work with a ready-made PTA cake. 'Storm's brewing,' she chuckled.

Another wave coming, I wrapped myself in kelp, grasping it tightly, not knowing how strong the sea would be, feeling like a fool, as it crashed into me. I found a place for my feet and squatted there, clinging to the thick rubbery strands. In the breaks between waves I began to knot. I remembered when the baby ran nappy-less in the first sun of spring, my veg plot had stirred, and as the green shoots poked through, they had spread up me too, a crisp menthol awakening. Growing and eating and selling what I could to the café up the road, I dreamt about a family restaurant.

Marjorie from work carried her cake into the kitchen, bending down to pick up the eggbox, innocently flashing a well packed thigh. 'I don't like that cake,' said Olive, flicking her eyes at Marjorie's, picking out a lump from the spill and moving it towards her lips. You whipped out a charming smirk for Marjorie from work, who was taking it all in.

'Let's make yours too then,' she said to Olive, rolling her eyes to you.

The next wave only hit my knees. So I waited as Belinda played her games, the sky whirled away, the sea had some fun, knowing you were right about the goddamned seaweed idea. We'd been to Scotland to visit my aunt, with my new minty eyes I saw seaweed on the menu. 'Seaweed. Our bay is full of it. Already grown, just think!' You and she smiled your encouraging smiles, I reddened at your acknowledging wink. Back home you'd said, 'Don't be crazy. No-one eats seaweed down here.'

Marjorie from work expertly mixed and quarter-filled the lined sandwich tins. Olive left to lick the bowl, you retreated for tea, while she spat it back in. On the sofa, a cautious complaint, a first fallen morsel, started the avalanche of soothing, comforting, massaging murmurs in that shared condition of yours. Marjorie certainly was the full package: cake-making, money-making, easy on the eye and the hand. She would be everything and **this** would be the real thing.

But Belinda had only been messing, and as she let the sea subside I unhooked myself; cold, pelleted and aching, shaking, pale skin thin but still alive. She tittered as I scrambled my way upwards; the beach was green with leafweed. Harvest enough for a restaurant, harvest enough for a feast.

Marjorie from work was already clearing up, the morsels in the milk swiped from the surface. The slim cake done, Olive sang sweetly, 'The first slice is for Marjorie!' Gilded flashes in both of your eyes. As she took her first bite and the salt engulfed her sides, Marjorie gulped and smiled.

'Too late, lovey,' she whispered. 'The deal's already done,' placing a hand on your thigh.

The carp whisperer

Petra McQueen and Katy Wimhurst

As Takiki drove away from the dry dust of her village, her hands sweated on the steering wheel. In the stationary queue to the ring road, she checked she could not be seen then spread out her fingers to let the breeze play. Only in these moments of absolute privacy did she allow herself this freedom. The childhood taunt, 'Takiki's a freakiky', could still make her feel shame about the webbing stretching from finger to finger.

The car behind her blared its horn, and she snapped her fingers together as though caught in crime.

'Alright! Alright!' she yelled and crawled onto the ring road. If she was late, she'd be fired and then what? About to work herself into a panic, she saw a billboard at the side of the road and managed a smile. Grey-haired folk waved from the doorsteps of quaint cottages, like they'd found a slice of heaven. Behind them, stretching up to the corner of the poster, were patchwork fields of fruit and vegetables with a river snaking through them. The legend, written in white across the clean blue sky, read: *eDen Island, D-class Retirement Homes.*

Auntie Letitia had signed up for a place at eDen as soon as Takiki had found her job in the city over a year ago. Six months later she was gone. I'll write again tonight, Takiki thought. But she knew the letter, and all the ones she'd written over the months, couldn't be sent until the postal service was up and running. God knows when that would be. When the rains fell again, perhaps, when the world started working the way it should.

At Lot 17, she scanned the tarmac for a space. There! As she pulled in, a strange light rippled along her car. She lifted her head to the lorry directly opposite her. Through its open door she could see rows of glass tanks filled with clean blue water. It was as if she'd fallen into a dream, a time from the past when such things had been possible.

She looked around expecting to see A-Quantrol Guards with machine guns protecting the precious cargo. When she saw none, only D-workers walking with bowed heads to the checkpoint, she leaped out of her car and onto the burning tarmac before she could stop herself. She lifted her face to the water. It was so clean, so blue, except... there! A flash of colour... Another. Gold and red and silver. What the hell was that?

'You took your time.'

She jumped. The owner of the voice appeared from inside the lorry, a Thor baton dangling from his belt. In his hand, he held a clipboard.

She took a step back. 'I'm sorry. I didn't mean to—'

'Well, you're here now.' When he came closer, she knew, from his deeply tanned skin and broad nose, that he wasn't an A-qua, nor a B-class, or even a C. He was a D-class worker just like her. But still a man with a Thor baton, a man who had caught her staring at the water.

He tucked the clipboard under his arm and she spied the picture at the top: a thin-faced young woman like her, with long braids and dark skin. 'You kept me waiting for half an hour.' He twisted his head to read the name on the board. 'Lola Burken.'

She was about to tell him she wasn't who he thought she was, when a big fish, golden-red, twitched its tail against the side of a tank. The man moved closer, and she had to wrench her eyes from the sight of the fish to listen. 'This was a stupid place to pick you up,' he said, 'too many low-lifes. Mate of mine was knifed for one of these buggers not so long ago. *And* I had to switch off the aircon to save on gas. If any of the koi are dead, you'll be going straight back.'

Koi? Was that what they were? She'd thought they were extinct. In her village, the lakes and ponds had given their water to the sky and in the hollows, black mud cracked, turned hard as brick. Now she saw that in some other place – eDen maybe? – there was water enough for a fish not to be eaten but cared for in swells.

'Come on up,' said the man, and tossed her an ID pass. Without even glancing at it, she slung it around her neck. He pulled the door shut behind them and the only light came from the tanks. She didn't think to be afraid of the man in the enclosed space, saw only the water and the fish with their sunset colours: red, orange, gold and silver. The webs of her fingers pulsed oddly.

The man plunged his hand into a tank and reached for a thermometer lying on the bottom. Not looking at her, he said, 'Don't just stand there. Do the rest. Gotta be 37.5C.'

The world tilted a little as she lifted a tank flap. With the very tips of her fingers she touched the water and found it cool and soft, like no water she'd ever known. She wanted to plunge in, let it rush over her face, work its way into her braids, lift each follicle. She snaked her hand towards the thermometer.

And then, then, the fish came.

It was as long as her forearm, fat and sleek. She twisted her hand, and it settled its belly in her palm. Out of the carp's mouth came a grape-sized bubble. She was so close she saw herself reflected in the sheen: her black face, the wide eyes. Another bubble rose and this time Takiki shone gold. The final reflection showed only the fish, inside the bubble, swishing its tail.

'You done there, missy?' said the man. 'Don't you worry your head about the rest of them. Good old Jack, heh, doing your work for you.' He walked out of the lorry and jumped to the ground. 'Act sharp, girl. We're already late, thanks to you.'

As though still caught in the fish's bubble, without a thought about what she was about to do, Takiki joined him in the front of the cab. It was only as they drove away and they passed the D-workers waiting at the checkpoint that the bubble popped. That was where she should be; not here in a lorry-load of fish. She studied the man out of the corner of her eye, working up courage to tell him to stop and drop her off, when she noticed a tattoo peeking out from his shirt cuff. Her hand slid off the door handle. The tattoo was of a Fire Serpent. Only D-gangsters had those. What kind of strings had he pulled to get a job like this?

The man shot her a glance. 'You looked about to jump,' he said. 'I know it's tough when you first get back, but you need to keep your shit together, focus on the end game. Am I right or am I right?'

She forced herself to nod, afraid to ask what he was talking about, admit that she had no right to be there. She'd heard stories of the revenge this type of man would take: beatings and stabbings. Worse even: so bad she wouldn't name them.

They stopped at the checkpoint to the inner city, a place Takiki had never been before, never would have been allowed. An A-Quantrol Guard walked towards them, a semi-automatic in his hands. As he reached over to accept the man's papers through the open window, he saw Takiki and raised his gun. Takiki shrank back in her seat.

'Hold it,' said the man. He stabbed at a piece of paper. 'Legit 529, special circumstances. We got here a Carp Whisperer.'

A Carp Whisperer? Hadn't she heard of that before? She delved into her memory and emerged on a night so hot that even the stars and the moon seemed to sweat. Sleep was impossible and she had called out for a story. With a pile of sewing on her knee, Auntie Letitia had told her a tale of a people who talked with carp.

'Why would they want to?'

'Carp are fishy clever, they listen and watch. A person who can talk to them will learn things. Not only that...' She put down her sewing. 'Carp Whisperers can shape-shift too.'

Takiki hitched up in bed. 'What's that?'

'Turn from person to fish and back again. But it has to be for a good reason, not just because they fancy it. They must first learn something so important that they have to swim back to their people to tell it.' She leaned over and stroked Takiki's hair. 'You, with those beautiful hands, maybe you have the fish magic. Sleep now.'

When she'd left, Takiki thought of the fish magic for a long while, then decided Aunt Letitia was trying to make her feel less like a freak. This story was nothing but an old wives' tale, something to whittle away the night, and she'd packed it away.

She lifted her head, to shake the memory and saw, for the first time, the trees which lined the road. They were sun-scorched and twisted but majestic, alive. She'd never seen so many together. She swivelled in her seat to take in the white marble buildings, the window boxes bursting with reds and yellows.

'We play the game right,' said the man, with a grin, 'we'll be living in one of those fancy apartments soon as dammit. I got my eye on one down Perch Avenue. Two more years and then I'm owed.'

Was that true? Could this job lead to that? A D-class man in the A-qua sanctum? No. The man was a fantasist, a dreamer, to think such a thing was possible. The best people like them could hope for was an extra litre or two of rations, and the promise of eDen Island when they retired.

A slip road took them to some steel gates manned by four A-Quantrol Guards with semi-automatics and sunglasses. The man waved his papers, and they were let through into a tunnel. The lorry shuddered as the engine died. 'Let's get to it.'

As she clambered down, the air smelled cool, of water. She'd thought that she'd be even more afraid at their destination, but there was a fluttering in her gut, an excitement. She ran over to the back of the lorry and watched as the man stepped up and unhooked a trolley from the side. 'Your friend first,' he said. She got in beside him and together they unclipped the clasps that held the tank to the wall and lifted it onto the trolley. The carp swished its panic. 'Calm it down, for God's sake,' said the man. 'I had one die from fright last month.'

She stared at him.

'Speak to it – that's your job, isn't it?'

She wanted to say that she didn't have the words, that this had been a terrible case of mistaken identity, but as the carp splashed, a rhythmic throb started in her gut. She clamped her hand on her belly as it coursed up through her throat and bubbled out of her mouth, a sing-song chant, deep and soft.

'That's it,' said the man when the carp settled and nosed itself towards the music. She stared at it, a bubble of joy in her chest. 'Keep going,' he said.

She would, she could. Crouched over the tank as it was pushed, she sang to it... no, with it: its gills pumped tiny spheres of air, words which were not quite words, yet Takiki found she understood. *All I am, you are too.*

Oh, oh, how well it sang, how clever it was.

We are water, we are life.

The song died as the man stopped to key in numbers on a huge metal gate. Takiki put her hand on the tank, wanting the koi to continue. *Sing to me.*

The fish made no response, even as it was pushed into the sun and the tarmac gave way to a slick marble path beneath Takiki's feet. *Please sing.* Nothing. Just a twitch of its tail. Takiki felt its silence as a strange sensation of cool air just behind her ears. Keeping her eyes on the fish, she lifted her hands and explored a welt, soft at the edges as though a cut had healed.

'Quite something, isn't it?' said the man.

She dropped her hands, afraid both of what she had felt and of the man discovering it. The man wasn't looking at her but at the view.

She stood straight, the thought of the welt knocked away by the view. They were standing in a wide open space in what must be the heart of the city. It was as big as her village and filled with ornamental ponds, small lakes and fountains, some linked by narrow, man-made streams. Pale stone walkways, lined by tubs of pink and blue flowers, criss-crossed the space and the hot sun danced in diamonds on the water.

'That apartment I've got my eye on,' said the man, 'is behind that building.' He pointed into the distance where a fringe of white balconies faced a lake. 'Imagine waking up every day and smelling this damn beauty of a place.'

She thought of it and of her village where the cracked ground burned the soles of the children's feet. 'Where are all the people?'

He paused. 'It's like... they don't know how lucky they are. Hardly any of them use it 'cept at weekends.'

'All this water. Is there...' She furrowed her brow, trying to remember the word, 'a spring here?'

'Nah, pipes bring it from the old wells north of the city.'

She took a step back and he must've seen what she was thinking because his mouth went tight. 'Keep your trap shut about this place outside work.'

She stared at him.

'I mean it, girl. The A-quas get even a whiff of you blabbing and you're in serious shit.' He ran a thumbnail across his throat as if slitting it. 'Two more years, I've got, two more. I don't need no trouble.'

She took a deep breath. 'Okay, I get it.'

He searched her eyes and gave a curt nod. 'You wait with the fish. I'll go and sort out the paperwork.'

She watched him walk down a path and vanish through some glass doors. By her side, the carp slapped the water with its tail, and, as though its song was in her head, she heard, *It's yours, it's yours.*

The song hummed in her head and belly, thrummed her fingers, behind her ears. She moved without wanting to and found herself at the edge of the ornamental pond. Her legs obeyed the song and she squatted, tilting her head to where the water rippled with a soft current. Her chest constricted, and for a moment the song stopped.

Just like the man had said, there was a dark wide hole in the wall where fronds waved as water streamed gently through. She pictured the pipe snaking beneath the white marble houses and guarded city wall, under the ring road, across the scrublands, and then further out to the arid hills and to the villages. Her village.

The song began again, high and piercing, *It's yours.* She stared at the pond glittering with sunlight and tried not to listen. But the song was inside her and her throat was dry as parched tarmac.

It belongs to you, to your people.

Her webs twitched and the strange cuts behind her ears throbbed as she knelt and pressed her face into the water. She gulped cool water and it slicked down her dry throat.

Take care!

From nowhere, the man was by her side. Before she could leap away, her hand was wrenched up her back. 'What the hell are you playing at?' His calloused hand burned on her wrist as he twisted her round to look at him. 'They'll send you back there. Only this time you'll be on the receiving end.'

Her eyes were fixed on the Thor Baton: one zap she'd be unconscious, two dead.

'Don't you think I get thirsty too?' he spat. 'But I'm not such a fool: I'm never going back to eDen.'

Takiki's world narrowed to a tunnel, the man at one end and her at the other. 'eDen?'

He shook his head. 'Don't give me that. You sanitised the olds too.' A vein pulsed on his neck. 'We had no choice, did we? Natural resources have to be conserved.'

As Aunt Letitia waved her hanky from the window of the mini-bus to eDen Island, she'd been going to her death. Not just her, but most of the olds from the villages. Why? Because they weren't even worth their three litres a day? Better to use their rations to fill a pond, have another cherub spewing water.

She tried to wriggle free, but the man was too strong. Beside her the carp flashed, slapping its tail. *Free yourself.* The man held the baton out to her neck and his thumb shook a little over the button. 'Stop struggling,' he commanded.

As she closed her eyes, the song rang within her. *Be brave. Be free.* She jerked her wrist and opened her fingers, spreading the webs wide. As he saw the strange pale flesh, his grip faltered.

There was no thought as she ran: only thick muscles under her glistening skin, only the smell of the water and the song humming in her veins. *We are water. We are life.* With once last glance at the man standing, Thor-baton in hand, she hurled herself over the side-wall of the pond

In the air she was skin and bone, limbs and lungs; as the water met her, she felt herself shrink, become dense, packed and powerful. Her legs jerked and fused; her flesh became sinew and scales. Gills opened, a tail swished, a sleek body slid. She twisted her spine, flicked her fins and in front of her was the blank gaping hole of the pipe. She was a fleeting streak of red-gold heading upstream back to her village. She would sing out the news to her people. *We are water. We are life. Resist. Be free.*

Populists are on the rise...

Chantal Mouffe

Populists are on the rise but this can be a moment for
progressives too

*Neoliberalism has created genuine grievances, exploited by the
radical right. The left must find a new way to articulate them.*

These are unsettled times for democratic politics. Shocked by the
victory of Eurosceptic coalitions in Austria and in Italy, the
neoliberal elites – already worried by the Brexit vote and the
victory of Donald Trump – now claim democracy is in danger and
raise the alarm against a possible return of 'fascism'.

There is no denying that western Europe is currently witnessing
a 'populist moment'. This arises from the multiplication of anti-
establishment movements, which signal a crisis of neoliberal
hegemony. This crisis might indeed open the way for more
authoritarian governments, but it can also provide the opportunity
for reclaiming and deepening the democratic institutions that have
been weakened by 30 years of neoliberalism.

Our current post-democratic condition is the product of several
phenomena. The first one, which I call 'post-politics', is the

blurring of frontiers between right and left. It is the result of the consensus established between parties of centre-right and centre-left on the idea that there was no alternative to neoliberal globalisation. Under the imperative of 'modernisation', social democrats have accepted the diktats of globalised financial capitalism and the limits it imposes on state intervention and public policies.

Politics has become a mere technical issue of managing the established order, a domain reserved for experts. The sovereignty of the people, a notion at the heart of the democratic ideal, has been declared obsolete. Post-politics only allows for an alternation in power between the centre-right and the centre-left. The confrontation between different political projects, crucial for democracy, has been eliminated.

This post-political evolution has been characterised by the dominance of the financial sector, with disastrous consequences for the productive economy. This has been accompanied by privatisation and deregulation policies that, jointly with the austerity measures imposed after the 2008 crisis, have provoked an exponential increase in inequality.

The working class and the already disadvantaged are particularly affected, but also a significant part of the middle classes, who have become poorer and more insecure.

In recent years, various resistance movements have emerged. They embody what Karl Polanyi presented in *The Great Transformation* as a 'countermovement', by which society reacts against the process of marketisation and pushes for social protection. This countermovement, he pointed out, could take progressive or regressive forms. This ambivalence is also true of today's populist moment. In several European countries those resistances have been captured by rightwing parties that have articulated, in a nationalistic and xenophobic vocabulary, the demands of those abandoned by the centre-left. Rightwing populists proclaim they will give back to the people the voice that has been captured by the 'elites'. They understand that politics is always partisan and requires an us/them confrontation. Furthermore, they recognise the need to mobilise the realm of emotion and sentiment in order to construct collective political identities. Drawing a line between the 'people' and the 'establishment', they openly reject the post-political consensus.

Those are precisely the political moves that most parties of the left feel unable to make, owing to their consensual concept of politics and the rationalistic view that passions have to be excluded. For them, only rational debate is acceptable. This explains their hostility to populism, which they associate with demagogy and irrationality. Alas, the challenge of rightwing populism will not be met by stubbornly upholding the post-political consensus and despising the 'deplorables'.

It is vital to realise that the moral condemnation and demonisation of rightwing populism is totally counterproductive – it merely reinforces anti-establishment feelings among those who lack a vocabulary to formulate what are, at core, genuine grievances.

Classifying rightwing populist parties as 'extreme right' or 'fascist', presenting them as a kind of moral disease and attributing their appeal to a lack of education is, of course, very convenient for the centre-left. It allows them to dismiss any populists' demands and to avoid acknowledging responsibility for their rise.

The only way to fight rightwing populism is to give a progressive answer to the demands they are expressing in a xenophobic language. This means recognising the existence of a democratic nucleus in those demands and the possibility, through a different discourse, of articulating those demands in a radical democratic direction.

This is the political strategy that I call 'left populism'. Its purpose is the construction of a collective will, a 'people' whose adversary is the 'oligarchy', the force that sustains the neoliberal order.

It cannot be formulated through the left/right cleavage, as traditionally configured. Unlike the struggles characteristic of the era of Fordist capitalism, when there was a working class that defended its specific interests, resistances have developed beyond the industrial sector. Their demands no longer correspond to defined social groups. Many touch on questions related to quality of life and intersect with issues such as sexism, racism and other forms of domination. With such diversity, the traditional left/right frontier can no longer articulate a collective will.

To bring these diverse struggles together requires establishing a bond between social movements and a new type of party to create a 'people' fighting for equality and social justice.

We find such a political strategy in movements such as Podemos in Spain, La France Insoumise of Jean-Luc Mélenchon or Bernie Sanders in the US. This also informs the politics of Jeremy Corbyn, whose endeavour to transform the Labour party into a great popular movement, working 'for the many, not the few', has already succeeded in making it the greatest left party in Europe.

Those movements seek to come to power through elections, but not in order to establish a 'populist regime'. Their goal is to recover and deepen democratic institutions. This strategy will take different forms: it could be called 'democratic socialism', 'eco-socialism', 'liberal socialism' or 'participatory democracy', depending on the different national context. But what is important, whatever the name, is that 'democracy' is the signifier around which these struggles are articulated, and that political liberal institutions are not discarded.

The process of radicalising democratic institutions will no doubt include moments of rupture and a confrontation with the dominant economic interests. It is a radical reformist strategy with an anti-capitalist dimension, but does not require relinquishing liberal democratic institutions.

I am convinced that in the next few years the central axis of the political conflict will be between rightwing populism and leftwing populism, and it is imperative that progressive sectors understand the importance of involving themselves in that struggle.

The popularity in the June 2017 parliamentary elections of Mélenchon, François Ruffin and other candidates of La France Insoumise – including in Marseille and Amiens, previous strongholds of Marine Le Pen – shows that when an egalitarian discourse is available to express their grievances, many people join the progressive struggle. Conceived around radical democratic objectives, populism, far from being a perversion of democracy – a view that the forces defending the status quo try to impose by disqualifying as 'extremists' all those who oppose the post-political consensus – constitutes in today's Europe the best political strategy for reviving and expanding our democratic ideals.

(This article was first published in The Guardian on Monday 10 September 2018.)

Fenner

Suzy Norman

Who knew time could be so malleable? When I was a little girl, time stretched ahead in one straight line like a skipping rope pulled tight, or at least that how it seemed to me. None of us could have predicted the scientific breakthrough which would upend it all.

Producer Dewi McInnery had written to inform me he planned to make a film about my late husband, Ray Harkus. A musician who was, in his words, a glorious and irrefutable cult God.

Ray had been my husband for nine years. Nine years and 254 days, to be exact. He died a decade ago, a windy August Thursday. I remember the sun was as hot as Grandma's oven. The wind cut through me the same way Grandma's nails used to scratch at my skin when she grabbed me, pulling me around the kitchen as she was wont to do. I remember it was the same day Prince William died. Nobody, least of all me, could have predicted him dying before he'd a chance to be king. I can't recall now how I felt about it. I mean, I wasn't sure who stunned me more in their passing, Ray or William.

In his letter, Dewi informed me, being as ten years had passed, he thought now would be an opportune time to pay tribute to his hero in celluloid form. He asked if I would assist him by agreeing to an interview.

I am fearful of interviews. I have somehow managed to avoid the journalists' persuasive letters, and the film-makers' sensitive, but nonetheless tenacious requests, but I made an exception for Dewi. It was a straight-forward request. I wouldn't say polite, but there was a force behind it. Rather than email me, he'd taken the trouble to write to me, a snail mail, and I read between the lines in that small and elegant writing you rarely see these days, that my acceptance was a given. At least that's how it seemed to me.

With this in mind, and prone as I am to indulge the whims of ambitious men, I made a decision. I photocopied his letter and filed the copy carefully away in a drawer. As for the original, I flared up a lighter and watched the corners blacken and curl until they became burnt mammocks floating.

Fading

Faded

Gone.

Sitting at Grandma's writing bureau, I wrote a response. In large spidery writing, I promised Dewi a friendly reception. I would prepare for him something special: smoky Japanese tea and a tricolour of small cakes – what's more I instructed him to make his way over the following day, a pleasantly-forecast Sunday.

I wait by the window at the top of the staircase and watch fronds of grey crack the path. I would like the sun to be a bit bolder to make me feel braver. Folding my arms across my chest to keep warm, I watch him slide into view. He approaches with his camera hidden away in a black case, as if this affords him an air of mystery. Cockily, he flicks open the gate and makes his way down the dark and glossy path, treacherous in the night's rain. It is when he reaches the first gravestone that I see how tall he is. He must be six of grandpa's headstones, all piled up to heaven.

Approaching the house, he moves his eyes over my red door until he spots the buzzer, but he stays motionless for a moment. Instead of pressing, he pulls up the hood of his anorak and heads around the back to see for himself a little of what I tantalised him with in my letter. He will have expected Fenner to be grander, more Gothic, I'm sure.

Quickly, I pull up my long skirt and run over to the back window, almost treading on Jack as I go. Jack hisses at me and and sears me with narrow, green eyes. He slides down the stairs, like one of those slinky toys I used to play with as a girl, a long, long time ago.

He passes the first pear tree that is throbbing with life now under a low, gold sun. The sun has somehow, in the few seconds it has taken me to run from East to West, escaped the clouds. He looks swiftly left, then right and smiles.

My toes brush the hem of my plain, white cotton skirt. I wonder if he looks up to see me, what he will make of me, old as I am now, my wavy greying hair running freely down my back. So thrilled to meet you, he'll say, whether he means it or not. Suddenly, I long to hear his voice.

By the gravestones at the back of the house, he strokes his freshly-shaved chin. It's true: the gravestones are solemn, cold, and not at all how I described them in my letter. He stands at the foot of Grandpa's grave. Grandma told me if I stood on his grave long enough, I'd grow taller. I want to tell Dewi this.

He moves away from the headstone and over to the pond. All is still. I can see from my vantage point there is not so much as a sliver of orange beneath the surface. The goldfish have been gone for some time now. Clouds gather again, blocking the sun. In this dirty light, the sludge on the surface of the pond is a dark, army green. Frogs rest by the edge, uninspired. Dewi looks up at the pear trees. My letter to Dewi had described Fenner in furious detail, my pen running away from me. I even told him how Ray liked to hang his underwear to dry on the tallest pear tree in the garden.

Afraid I'll be seen, I move to edge of the window. I close my eyes. For a moment, I hear laughing, smoky and deep. When I open them again, Dewi is gone and the buzzer trills. Descending the stairs to greet him, I still hear laughing. I see a flash of Ray's black hair. It had been a profound feeling the first time I saw Ray's hair, so profound I can still touch it in my memory. It was as if his hair was the colour of grief, even then.

I could never had predicted Ray would have been interested in me. I felt small in those days, more like a shadow than a fully grown woman of flesh. I was happy, so happy, to melt into the background; a woman of no consequence, Grandma said. Even Grandma's Cork accent, as rhythmic as the typewriter Grandpa hammered away at in his small reading room when he was writing another school report, was part of my happiness. An only child, I had all I needed. I had no desire for anyone to share my toys, or help me pick pears as ripe and swollen as the belly on Grandma's Jack Russell bitch who seemed to always be sleeping on the flagstone floor. The summer rain so constant it could melt your bones was exhilarating to me then. Every event from the heavens, large or small was part of my own heartbeat, and the heartbeat of Fenner, my home.

Dewi pulls the zip of his anorak down and looks at me, as if he's waiting, seeking my permission to speak. I smile warmly. He complains it's muggy, so I lift the window and the cold shoos in. He looks about him. From his shoulder bag he pulls out a soft, red notepad and smiles to see a photo of Ray centre shelf above the microwave. Ray's hair blows in the breeze, along with his sapphire tie. The only time I believe he ever wore one. I hold on to my flower headpiece. Confetti falls.

With his back to the window, he watches me boil the hob-top kettle. I watch his mouth open as if to speak. He studies pencil drawings pinned by magnets to the fridge door.

Something curious about them, no? I ask, embarrassed I'd forgotten to remove them in preparation. Your work is certainly interesting, but it's not to everyone's taste, Grandma warned me.

Now, would you like a drop of milk? I ask. Sugar?

No milk, one sugar, he says. Just a splash. A young niece is it? They're very good.

He explains he can't believe he's actually here in Ray's house. He tells me he's indebted to me and this pleases me. Taking our mugs with me, I lead him through to the living room where I invite him to set up his equipment. I like Welsh names, I tell him, and feel myself blushing.

Dewi is Welsh for David, he tells me. I feel myself shiver. Grandma always said David was an honest name.

As I sit opposite him on the sofa, I enjoy listening to new sounds in this old house: a leather bag unzipping, the swooshing sound of an anorak slung on the armchair, the hum of cables fizzing as he plugs them into the socket in the wall. From underneath my chair, I pull a selection of old photographs from a tin box and rest them on my lap.

Just put that there, I tell him, that's right. Forgive the mess. Just move that pile of books off the chair. No, no, that's right, put them there under the mantelpiece. Do you need another socket? There again, by your foot. Good good. Forgive me if I'm a little nervous, but I'm not used to visitors.

It's all new, this equipment, he tells me. I'm still getting to grips with it, he says. He pulls something silver from his case, it's long and wide. The sight of his camera makes me stiffen.

Don't be scared, he says. Just treat it as a friend.

Will that help? I ask nervously.

As his hazel eyes shrink in concentration, I see now there is a gloss of sweat around the receding line of his black hair. His hands are broad and capable as he presses the switch and turns the lens towards me.

It's not possible to live the life you dreamed of as a child, nobody can, I tell the lens. I can do this, I tell myself.

It's not possible to live a life you want by trying to make things happen. Everything is purely chance. Or luck, some might say. People think if you try and try to make something happen then some day it will, but I never believed this. I believe Ray was meant to find me and come to live here, although the knowing of it causes me to stop and wonder.

It's nearly ten years since he died, I say. My body was soft then, and I blew around like the pear trees in summer's wind, giddy with him and with the quiet life. We'd managed to fool them all, all the voices and pictures inside our smart phones, just disappeared back here to Ireland when Grandma died. It was perfect, and I felt like a mouse escaping the storm by hiding in Grandma's oven still warm from baking bread.

I glance from the lens to Dewi's torso, and back to the lens. I swallow.

It's funny, I say, but last night I drew Ray. Almond eyes. Arms strong. A narrow mouth lifted at the edges. I drew him as he was then, running his long fingers over the length of my breasts.

I run my own hand over my flat and sunken breasts. I want to keep talking, I *need* to.

Last night I ran a shower, I say, and so as to heat the tepid water as much as I could, I thought of him as he was the first time. Droplets of water slipped down my legs. I sprayed some shower gel and lathered it between my hands. I imagined his hands kneading my pocked thighs, kissing my coarse hair and gently lifting my sagging breasts with those hands I knew so well until I was writhing like a dying whale on the shore. I'd forgotten how it feels to... I'm sorry... Grandma said I was a true artist, as she saw it, because I was so open and...

As I stall and wonder whether to change my story or stop altogether I say this: it's this house, it's still the same but it's so empty now.

I look around me. The walls seem to darken. The room has never felt so small. The pipes howl with life and the roof sags above my head, as if filled with rain water, about to burst open and flood the room. Even as I fade into myself, I look at Dewi's hair and all I can see is black.

The flotsam boy

Steven O'Brien

The flotsam boy lay face down at the margin where sea and sand sucked against each other, amid shreds of carrageen and bladderwrack. The soles of his neatly-buckled sandals and his Sunday-best blue shorts and red shirt were drying slowly. His face was half in the shush of the drawing water, as if he were sleeping on the shoulder of his mother. Down by his side the palms of his hands were open to the morning.

This is how the old man Parthalan found him, after the midsummer night storm had blown itself out. Starfish, crabs and dogfish purses were laced along the tidemark. And this boy cast up among scraps of net and oily wood. Parthalan walked across the beach with a crown of screeching herring gulls at his head. When the birds caught sight of the boy they flew down to step on the sand in a wide quarrelling circle. The old man waved his blackthorn stick and the birds once more took the lift of wind and their cursing cries were like broken glass to his ears.

His trousers were patched over and patched again. His fingers were knobbed and white. His face was like a chunk of grey feldspar. His hair was the colour of the long dull clouds that wrapped along the cliffs of the island for forty weeks a year. But today the sun was high and far off, out at sea, the wind turbines were glancing slowly as they wheeled in the blue.

Parthalan had been alone for a long time. His surprise at seeing the boy on the white sand was an old man's surprise – cautious, reckoning, slow. He bent over the boy and his bony elbows poked through two identical holes in the sleeves of his ganzie. He contemplated the golden skin of the half-nestled cheek; the soft lashes of one closed eyelid. He saw the brown curls, clean as those of a new calf. It was a good while before he stretched out his hand. Sea-slaked cold was the flesh of the boy. His shirt was clammy as a dishcloth.

Parthalan threw aside the blackthorn stick and turned the boy over. As he did so seawater ran freely from the little nose and mouth. He was as pliable and cold as a salmon. Parthalan picked a scrap of purple dulse from the boy's hair and then laid him out on his back. He sat down then beside the body and spent a long hour looking down at the quiet brown face while the distant turbines slowly trimmed the dawn sunlight.

Behind him were steep banked grassy dunes and then the flower strewn machair stretching up to the foot of the mountains. In these northern islands warmth is rare and never lasts for long. So it was the passing of the morning into shadow that stirred Parthalan. Slowly but with an obvious sense of purpose, he got to his feet. He lifted the boy. The cold face fitted into the crook of his neck. The buckled sandals dangled against his chest. He turned and sloughed up the dunes.

A skylark high above old Parthalan looked down on an island with no roads, no village, no shop. Just a stone hut under two yew trees. It had a tin roof and a flaked blue door swinging in the wind.

In the hut was an iron bed, a table and a chair. On a shelf was one cup, a tin jug, a set of cutlery and a plate – all dull and dented. Parthalan laid the boy on the bed, then stood scratching his beard.

The yew trees outside creaked against each other in the breeze with a dry sawing. And this was also the sound of the old man's voice, when he finally spoke, for he had not done so in a very long time.

He brushed away grains of sand from the dead boy's face. 'I wove the island all around with a dark sleep, so that none could see it, and none could approach.' He arranged the boy's golden limbs and put his hand on his forehead. 'But here is sea sorrow come, in this little death.'

He bent to reach under the bed and with both hands he drew out a bundle wrapped in oilskin. Sitting back on the stool he placed the weight of the bundle on his knees. He unfurled it to reveal a book something like a church bible. The cover was split and weathered as ancient walnut bark. For a while his fingers passed over the leather. When finally he opened the book his hand trembled. Most of the pages had been ripped away.

'You were a proud tome once, but like an old friend met again by chance, I scarcely know you now.' He laughed quietly, but he didn't smile.

Parthalan went through the scraps of vellum. 'So much is lost... and that is for the better,' he said. 'Yet surely there is something here.' The old man traced his fingertip through webs of scrawling diagrams until it seemed that half his hand was paddling in them. Abruptly he closed the book and looked across his shoulder. Then he sucked in the wind between the gaps in his teeth and waited.

A figure came in through the door; a figure made of the lick of moonlight on a rock pool. A figure of parts that could fold itself flat and then draw up to the corner of the roof, and after fall across the floor like a spilt purse of silver shillings.

'I am here,' its voice was the wind pressing through the yew trees outside.

'Long time' said Parthalan. He scarcely tried to follow the constant shift and poise of the figure around the stone walls.

'Not for me,' it said.

'Look,' said the old man. He placed his hand on the moss-filled mattress on which the boy lay.

'I see him,' breezed the figure. 'I saw him.'

'Of course – you are everywhere.' Once more Parthalan touched the child's forehead. 'I know there must be a freight of grief here, but I don't understand it.'

'I would have pity if I were human.'

'You said something like that once before.' Parthalan was looking straight ahead but he saw the figure twist in a shaft of sunshine at the corner of his eye.

'Well then, do not think I am changed.' Its voice was like the distant rush of a mill race.

Parthalan's left thumb had been in the book all the while. It looked like he was going to open it again but now he paused. 'You have listened at every keyhole for as long as men have had doors. Tell me, what are the tall white gyres in the sea?'

'Ha!' the figure cried. 'Ponder how much the world has turned since you shut yourself away and how much you have lost. Those white spokes provide a force to people on the mainland that you would think is magic. And this magic is not called up by doddering gimmers incanting spells.'

'You have a bitter tongue.' Parthalan looked down at his knees and shook his head as he digested what the figure had said. His face looked very old.

The figure shifted to a fleeting glint on the ring Parthalan's wore on his left hand. 'Yes my voice has sherbet in it, sharp as moon ice, but I do not lie. Where is *your* tall pride? Where is *your* beautiful magic?'

'There's not much left of either.'

'So why have you called down me from *everywhere*?'

'Because I must use the last dregs and I need you.' For a second the figure was a flicker on the buckle of the dead boy's sandal but as Parthalan turned his head the gleam cut loose to rest itself on the window latch.

'I am at your shoulder. You *need* me?' In the hut there was laughter. 'This is new. I am not bound anymore. Why should I assist?'

'Because you came. Because you can.' Parthalan's tone was somewhere between anger and desperation.

The voice hissed behind his chair. 'So I'll stay, but you must understand, this is my choice.'

'Whatever you say, just bide and watch.'

'And then I will go.' The figure settled itself on the lip of the tin jug on the shelf.

'As you wish.' As Parthalan opened his book once more the bindings creaked. He was silent as he spread his fingers across the nonagons, pentadecagons and scribbles. After a while he sucked the wind between his teeth again and waited.

In no more than a minute the dead boy convulsed and began hacking up gouts of salty water. The retching increased. His little knees drew up to his chin. Then his back arched. He flailed his arms. Yet Parthalan sat silently by the bed until he saw the boy's eyelids begin to flicker.

'Quick,' he cried, 'his soul is still five fathoms drowned. Go and lead him from the deep.'

'I am made of cool fire,' replied the figure. 'I will be a lure in the black labyrinth of his death.'

Parthalan tore the scrap of spells from his book and cast it aside. Then he bent forward and opened the boy's eyes. He looked down into the wet inky grotto of sleep and he saw a shimmer twisting up from far below. Suddenly the boy sat up and vomited water all over the front of the old man's ganzie. There was a seesaw of light as the figure leaped from the boy's dark pupils and glanced all round the hut. The boy began to cry and stutter the word 'Dayik, Dayik' over and over.

'I am at your shoulder,' the figure said. 'Rushing up from that void was a joy, but I must be gone now. He is calling for his mother.'

'Wait,' said Parthalan as he rocked the boy. 'You know his language. Talk to him. Ask him his story.'

'I yearn for the endless sky. I must be away.'

'Please,' Parthalan's voice was dry and low.

'I delight in your entreaty.' (Again the birdsong laughter).

'Then please' repeated the old man, 'sit and question the boy with me.'

'Very well. I shall be in your mouth and at the gate of your ear.'

Parthalan sat the boy back on the mattress and softly he began to speak to him, his old voice overlaid by the creature of light. Between sniffling and wiping his nose, the boy began to reply.

'What is your name?' asked Parthalan, holding the boy's hand.

'I can't remember,' said the boy and although his language was strange the figure translated everything. Indeed, the boy appeared to think that Parthalan was speaking directly to him.

'Then tell me what you do remember about how you came here.'

The boy thought for a while. His eyes were big and very dark. At last his words poured out 'Yellow mountains. We had never seen the sea... We left when war was near... war was always close but one night Father said we should go... Mother wanted to stay but when the roof caved in we had to run... Lorries and dust on the road... money for the soldiers... money for men in the night... everyone riding away, or walking... all the people in the sun... sisters taken from us and fire across a flat rocky plain and people broken like sticks and smashed pots... towns turned upside down... then the water.'

'Go on,' said Parthalan.

'A boat like a mountain above us... waves bigger than everything, rising and dizzying my legs... but the war was chasing us... People's voices from other places, with tangled words – my father told us they came from the south and all the world was running away – all the world... then a smaller boat and just me and my brothers and my father and my mother holding each other as the little boat tossed us up... and we were going to the safe shore... so I closed my eyes and held on and held on.'

Parthalan leaned forward and took the boy's hand. 'And then?'

The boy's eyes widened but his mouth worked silently for a moment. Quickly his voice grew into a wail, as if he was still foundering and crying out in the sea. 'And then...? And then...? And then sleep... cold sleep in the water!'

The boy began rocking back and forth and tears ran down his cheeks. He laid down slowly and went to sleep with the words 'Dayik, Dayik' on his lips.

One of the boy's tears fell to the floor but as it touched the cold flagstone it rose up higher and higher, taking on a human form with silver skin and glittering eyes. It addressed old Parthalan 'What are you doing?' It asked.

'Trying to find out.'

'For this child you have dragged back from death, or for yourself?'

Parthalan put his face in his hands. 'You are right,' he said. His fingers were in his beard as he sucked in the wind between his teeth. 'I just wished to know about the affliction of the world and why my spells could not keep my island free of them.'

'Have you used up all your magic?'

'Nigh on' said Parthalan. 'I see that my power has faded utterly.'

'So what will you do with him now?'

'I will do nothing. You must take him back into the world.'

The silver figure bent over Parthalan. 'Why should I take orders from you?' it said in a haughty voice. 'You released me from your service centuries ago and this boy will slow me in my endless flight.'

'Take him all the same.'

'But your book is empty. You are powerless to summon me ever again. You will fade and be forgotten.'

'Ah, it seems there are no pages in the book now – it is what I always wanted,' said Parthalan smiling. 'Don't you see what I have done? This is my gift to you, conjured with the very last of my magic. I have given you pity.'

The figure drew itself up to full height. Light flickered across its limbs and it sighed, 'I did not want this.'

'Pity weighs more than the boy. So take him,' said Parthalan. 'Take this little child and guard him. Try to find his family and if you cannot find them, watch over him until he grows to be a man.'

The creature of light sighed again. Then it gathered up the sleeping boy and departed. Parthalan hobbled after them and let fall his empty book in the grass.

The old man watched the silver figure rise above the waves in the strait and pass the turning blades of the wind turbines. The flotsam boy slept on.

Nature and culture

Jules Pretty

The Biodiversity and Cultural Diversity Complex

There is a widespread recognition today that the diversity of life involves both the living forms (biological diversity) and the worldviews and cosmologies of what life means (cultural diversity). These assets are so inextricably linked that one cannot exist without the other. Even when considered as a dichotomy, it is clear that nature and culture converge on many levels that span belief systems, social and institutional organisations, norms and knowledge, behaviours and languages. As a result, there exists mutual feedback between cultural systems and the environment, with shifts in one reciprocally leading to changes in the other. Thus the division sometimes made between nature and culture is in many cases a product of modern industrialised thought shaped by the need to control and manage nature.

Biodiversity is defined as the variation of life at the level of gene, species and ecosystem. Much has been written on its importance in terms of intrinsic value, human uses, and role in today's economies as well as providing livelihood options for resource-dependent communities worldwide. Biodiversity represents the product of thousands of years of evolution. At the same time, it serves as an absorptive barrier, providing protection from and resilience to environmental perturbations. All systems have limits of change (tipping points). Within these limits, systems can tolerate and adapt to shocks and stresses while still sustaining normal function. Going beyond thresholds, however, results in the destabilisation of the system. Biodiversity is now a recognised prerequisite to ecosystem health and resilience, as well as an essential precondition to sustainable livelihoods and human health.

Culture can be defined as the combination of practices, networks of institutions and systems of meanings. Cultural systems code for the knowledge, practices, beliefs, worldviews, values, norms, identities, livelihoods and social organisations of human societies. Different cultures value nature in different ways, so having different connections with their natural environments. The maintenance of cultural diversity into the future increases the capacity of human systems to adapt and cope with change. In the same way that biological diversity increases the resilience of natural systems, cultural diversity has the capacity to increase the resilience of social systems.

Beliefs, Cosmologies and Worldviews: Our Place in Nature

Many industrialised cultures have come to perceive nature and culture as two separate entities, with the prevailing modernist view tending to be of a nature-culture dichotomy in which people assert their dominance over nature. However, some cultures hold a more inclusive view perceiving humans as interdependent components of nature. In this case, nature is regarded as a force that manages human existence. In practice, the worldviews of human communities form a spectrum between these extremes.

What is more, perceptions of nature are dynamic and with the coming challenges of climate change and peak oil, it is conceivable that those communities whose livelihoods appear (on the surface) to be resource-independent, may have to undergo substantial changes in their perceptions and practices in the near future.

Many communities do not recognise a distinction between nature and culture, viewing themselves as part of the same continuum as the lands to which they belong. Although relationships/kinships with non-human entities (such as plant, animal, spirit and god) are easily observable, the relationship with nature is often more intrinsic and subtle, so that it goes unspoken and unrecognised. Thus to have a strong sense of oneness with nature is to not recognise a distinction between nature and culture. On the other hand, communities with a weak sense tend to perceive humans as separate from nature. E O Wilson conjectured that all humans, no matter their culture, have an innate connection with nature based on our common histories as hunter-gatherers. He termed this innate bond biophilia: 'a love of nature'. The idea of biophilia is widely supported by evidence that many people living in affluent urban areas still acknowledge a spiritual or affective relationship with nature and the outdoors.

Human Dominion and Nature

Human cultures and their associated behaviours shape biodiversity through the direct selection of plants and animals and the reworking of whole landscapes. Such landscapes can be described as anthropogenic nature: their composition, whether introduced species or agricultural monocultures, is a reflection of local culture and a product of human history, including the context in which individuals and groups live their lives. Food is an example of how human cultures shape and determine the composition of ecological landscapes. Food plays a role above and beyond nutrition in human societies; it helps to define our identity as individuals, societies and distinct cultures. Food also acts as a social marker, representing social structure and politics, as well as being used during religious and spiritual ceremonies. Food also epitomises how a culture uses, classifies and thinks about its natural resources, as such the diversity of diets today reflects the diversity of cultures that exist. Diets originally evolved from the resources available on the local landscape, and thus sustaining traditional diets, dishes and foods, acts to retain connections to both ancestors and the landscape.

Nature has been described as a cultural archive, a record of human endeavour and husbandry. Even ecologies previously thought to be natural and pristine are now known to be the result of long-term cultural interactions (e.g. resource dependent livelihood practices) according to recent archaeological and ethnographic evidence, negating the term and concept of wilderness. For this reason, many perceive landscapes to be a partial social construct, formed from the connection and interaction between people and place. Today, very few landscapes are non-human, except for the extremes of the poles or the depths of the oceans, although global climate change is bringing this assertion into question, acknowledged by the naming of this era as the *Anthropocene.*

Although natural resource-based practices and knowledge vary greatly between human cultures, and even between communities within the same culture, sustainable management systems often derive from the coexistence of culture when resource harvesting is coupled with environmental management. Community-based conservation is the process by which biodiversity is protected by the local community using their local knowledge and practices. Of course, not all livelihood activities developed by resource-dependent communities lead to high biodiversity. But in every traditional culture exists practice and knowledge, developed from worldviews, belief systems and livelihood dependencies, that can sustainably manage ecological integrity more successfully than modern affluent societies have hitherto managed.

Drivers of Diversity Loss and System Degradation

A healthy system is able to maintain full functionality in times of stress, and is thus resilient to incremental changes and perturbations. The diversity of a system is frequently used as a proxy for health, since a diverse system has more adaptive capacity and is therefore more likely to cope with change. However there have been unparalleled losses in biological and cultural diversity in recent decades. As a consequence, both human and ecological systems are becoming less stable (e.g. through the disruption of livelihoods, governance, resource pools and cultural traditions).

Many causes of biodiversity loss are also responsible for the loss of cultural diversity. Despite this, the loss of biodiversity is often considered as a separate policy issue to that of cultural diversity (e.g. through language loss or assimilation). Both have undergone an unprecedented rate of decline in recent decades, shifting towards monocultures of the land, people and mind. Common drivers of erosion include a shift in consumption patterns, the globalisation of food systems, and the commodification of natural resources. These drivers are reinforced by pressures of assimilation (attempting to integrate minority cultures into dominant society) and urbanisation, and are at their most damaging when they lead to rapid periods of socio-economic change, jeopardising local system resilience.

Extreme natural events comprise one of the most rapid drivers of change, particularly when coupled with anthropogenic stressors. Tools commonly used in externally-imposed resource management also create common drivers and threats, such as exclusive policies (for example in some nature-reserves or state-imposed systems). A lack of transboundary cooperation and geopolitical instability threaten global diversity, as do weak institutions and a lack of resources. Amplifying this is the widespread encroachment and reclamation of traditional lands in search of rapid economic returns.

The combination of social, economic and political drivers has led to global climate change and other environmental threats including overexploitation and habitat destruction, leading to unprecedented rates of species extinction. This erodes the resilience of human and ecological systems, particularly in resource dependent societies. The degradation of ecosystems with attendant issues of food security, spread of human pathogens, newly emerging and resurging infectious diseases, and the creation of psychological ills, is a major cause of ill-health today. Thus an unprecedented combination of pressures is emerging to threaten the health of human and ecological systems across the world, by forcing communities towards or over critical thresholds, leading to vulnerability and decline. These threats are paving the way to the growing homogenization of cultures and landscapes.

Story Telling

Local knowledge of nature is accumulated in a society and transferred through cultural modes, such as stories and narratives, as people travel over the land, spatially and temporally. It comprises a compilation of observations and understandings contained within social memory that try to make sense of the way the world behaves. Societies then use this collective knowledge to guide their actions towards the natural world. As a body of knowledge, it is rarely written down, enabling this cultural resource to remain dynamic and current, adapting with the ecosystem upon which it is based.

Alienation from nature has contributed to environmental problems in today's world. Until fairly recently in human history, our daily lives have been intertwined with living things. Now we are increasingly suffering from an extinction of experience. Observation today can bring much needed respect, and if we are lucky, we will find that animals, birds and places intercept us in our wanderings, helping to bring forth distinctive and personal stories of the land.

This story and knowledge creation from local circumstances has been called ecological literacy. Some have called this traditional knowledge, but this can be problematic – many moderns suspect it implies a backward step, knowledge that is only superstition. Traditional, though, is best thought of as not a particular body of knowledge, but the process of coming to knowing. Our lives involve the continuous writing and rewriting of own stories, by adjusting behaviour and by being shaped by local natures, and so our knowledges must be undergoing continuous revisions. Ecological or land literacy is not just what we know, but how we respond, how we let the natural world shape us and our cultures.

An acquisition process like this inevitably leads to greater diversity of cultures, languages and stories about land and nature because close observation of one set of local circumstances leads to divergence from those responding to another set of conditions. This is a critical element of knowledge for sustainability – its local legitimacy, its creation and recreation, its adaptiveness, and its embeddedness in social processes. This knowledge ties people to the land, and to one another. So when landscape is lost, it is not just a habitat or feature. It is the meaning for some people's lives.

Such knowledges are often embedded in cultural and religious systems, giving them strong legitimacy. This knowledge takes time to build, though it can be rapidly lost. Writing of American geographies, author Barry Lopez says, *'to come to a specific understanding... requires not only time but a kind of local expertise, an intimacy with a place few of us ever develop. There is no way round the former requirement: if you want to know you must take the time. It is not in books'.*

This tells us something about what ecological literacy really is. It is not just knowing the names of things and their functional uses (or values), but placing ourselves as humans as an intimate part of an animate, information-rich, observant and talkative world. They do not see the world as inanimate, with natural resources to be exploited, gathered, shot and eaten. These things are done, but only in certain ways, and the world is respected and treated with care. Indigenous people believe that if they cause harm to nature, then they will themselves come to harm, whether it is speaking without respect of certain animals, or whether it is over-fishing a lake or hunting out a certain type of animal. This is something that the industrialised world seems to have lost, and perhaps needs to remember. We have come to believe that harm to the world is inconsequential, or at the very least if something is lost then it can be replaced. We no longer think the consequences will come back to haunt us. When we stop listening and watching with care, our literacy about the world declines, and the landscapes no longer speak to us.

In *Wisdom Sits in Places*, Keith Basso says of the Apache groups, wisdom sits in places, and landscapes are never culturally vacant. Animals, places and whole landscapes have meanings, sometimes sobering, sometimes uplifting, but always with a moral dimension. Ecological literacy is not just about knowing, it is about knowing what to do, and when to do the right thing. Places and things *'acquire the stamp of human events'*, or memorable times, and people wrap these into stories that can be myths, historical tales, sagas or just gossip. Every story begins and ends with the phrase, *'it happened at...'*, and this anchoring of narrative to places means mention of a place evokes a particular story, which in turn carries a moral standard, and implication for certain types of social relations. Some Apache dialogues comprise only of a sequence of place names. After one such interaction, an elderly woman explained, *'we gave that woman a picture to work on in her mind. We didn't speak too much to her. We didn't hold her down'*.

What Next?

The notion of the inevitable benefits of all material progress is a modern invention. Hunters and foragers, many farmers and herders too, tend not to hold that their current community is any better than those of the past or at other places. Past and future are no more or less valued than current time. But economic development too easily justifies the losses of both species and special places, as we expect losses to be offset by creating something much better. Our environmental problems are thus human problems. Disconnection from the land, in the form of non-regular contact, already has the capacity to damage and even destroy cultures. Yet many talk of the need for escape, to get away from it all.

Something important remains elusive to many moderns in affluent countries. It is much happiness. We do not have clear answers, but the proportion of people in industrialised countries describing themselves as happy has not changed since the 1950s, despite a trebling of wealth. At the same time, the incidence of mental ill-health has grown rapidly. We solved, largely, infectious diseases; then came cancers. Our lives were extended and treatments improved; then came obesity, and problems of cardiovascular disease and diabetes. Dementias have become more common in the elderly. The reasons are largely simple: bad lifestyles, wrong foods, too little physical activity.

Evolutionary history is framed by losses and gains. The same goes for humans and our cultures. Ways of living emerged that were adapted to local ecosystems. Wild places, farms, grasslands, gardens: none were invariant. And whether hunter or farmer, we changed things, and in return our minds have been shaped by the land. Then came the industrial revolution, and the invention of machines that released abundant energy from coal. Within half a century, oil gushed from wells, and it changed the world yet again. Then consumer culture transformed the old equations about people and land. Global connectedness now illuminates the upsides of consumption, and aspirations are converging. But now come considerable environmental and social side-effects, so serious they threaten this finite planet's capacity to resource all our wants. Conventional economic growth encourages a race to the top of consumption, even though large numbers of people currently have no prospects of escaping poverty or hunger. We still call this progress.

Yet reason and evidence have not compelled us to care enough for nature. A good future will not be a return to something solely rooted in the past: we need medical, farm and transport technology, certainly computers and modern communications. But a hybrid vigour might be created through *both-and* practices rather than *either-or*. A new green economy in which material goods have not harmed the planet would be a good economy: even better if production processes could improve natural capital. The great majority of non-industrial cultures which maintain links to the land have done so through local cultural institutions, often manifesting in nature a variety of spiritual symbols and stories that command respect. If we wish to convince people to manage the planet sustainably and consume in different ways, then we will have to embed twenty-first century lifeways in a new texture of beliefs, emotions and experience. We will need moral teachings and wisdom about the environment and our duties as individuals. Through a different kind of consciousness of the world, perhaps our impact can be changed.

In such a barbarian green economy there would be regular engagements with nature, whether in gardens or wild places, city parks or fields, many people doing things together in rituals that make these behaviours valued and worth repeating, people giving to others and making intergenerational links, and communities investing time in activities that build contentment and well-being. We may need to break the current rules, bring the wilds inside the city walls, introduce new behaviours, create different aspirations.

There is some journeying to be done. Paths to be explored, and new ones made. Each year, the pine leans a little further. After night, the dawn comes. There is mud, but the birds are singing. The waves come and go, but the ocean is still there.

Bethlehem 16th May 2018

Mazin Qumsiyeh

I write from Bethlehem where 200,000 Palestinians have been squeezed into a canton, a ghetto, a *bantustan*, or an open air-prison surrounded by walls, less than 13% of the original district size of Bethlehem. Bethlehem has three refugee camps; 7.5 million of us are refugees or displaced people. Israel continues the ethnic cleansing started at its birth in 1948. But Bethlehem is still better than Gaza where a genocide is now practised. Before I continue, let me tell you that there are many signs both of the end of the human civilization and of its rejuvenation. These difficult times do test people's souls and minds, and while we find those who fail the test (like Netanyahu, Trump, Hagee, Mohammad *bin Salman*, and so on), we do find so many who pass it and light the way for us. The signs that this will not end well are manifold; they relate mostly to the behaviours of rogue regimes like Israel and the US: the withdrawal from climate change agreements, collapse of disarmament deals (first with Russia then with Iran), stealing a city from its people as a gift for immigrant European Jews and celebrating that theft (particularly horrible when it concerns that most sacred of cities – Jerusalem), the ongoing campaign of genocide directed against two million people (mostly refugees) in Gaza, and governments that no longer even pretend to care about human rights or international law. The US withdrawal from climate change agreements and the collapse of disarmament deals, first with Russia then with Iran add to these woes. I could go on. But there are also signs of hope and struggle.

My book, *Popular Resistance in Palestine: A history of Hope and Empowerment,* scans a part of our 130-year plus history of amazing resilience and success. Palestinians around me give me hope. The people of Gaza (maligned and misrepresented by the international media) give us hope. Today there is a total strike by millions of Palestinians living under Israeli occupation. My students give me hope. They and all young Palestinians are willing to sacrifice even their lives for the cause (they just need stronger leadership). I see hope in the Palestinians demonstrating in Jerusalem and in areas of Palestine occupied or/and colonized in 1948. I see it in the angry looks of Israeli colonial soldiers who rip flags out of civilian hands and beat people, frustrated that they are unable to colonize people's minds like they colonized their lands. And while governments in the mentally colonized Gulf States (Saudi Arabia and UAE) are silent, other people and other governments ACT. South Africa has pulled its ambassador from 'Israel' and so should other countries. People of all faiths act. Naturei Karta (Orthodox Torah Jews) demonstrated in Jerusalem together with their Christian and Muslim Jerusalemites against the imposter false prophets: Kushner, Freedman, Greenblatt, Netanyahu, and Hagee). Boycotts, Divestments, Sanctions will grow. I think people should also boycott and sanction the country that is 'the biggest purveyor of violence in the world'– in the words of Martin Luther King Jr – the USA.

More and more people are recognising Zionist propaganda for what it is in the so-called mainstream media. For example, CNN reports are couched in Zionist language; their interviews are mostly with Zionist politicians and US politicians who are Zionist. Their use of the language of omission betrays them: 'Dozens die in Gaza as US Embassy opens in Jerusalem'. Who died and who the killers were is not mentioned. We are told people die 'in clashes' at the borders of Israel and Gaza, but when unarmed civilian refugees are massacred as they demonstrate for their internationally recognised right to return to their homes and lands, then 'clashes' is a misleading term. In my view, the real story behind the blood bath of the past 24 hours, is how an American administration was persuaded to violate international law by relocating its embassy to stolen lands. It is the scandal of the massacre by Israeli apartheid forces of 60 unarmed civilians, many of whom were children – including an eight month old baby – and a double amputee. Over 2000 civilians were also injured, more than 700 with live ammunition.

The job

Martin Reed

Like many young people DeeTee lived, most of the time, in a world of his own. DeeTee's ownworld was rather like a 1980s rock album cover. There were two large moons, a baleful red-giant of a sun, lots of purple mountain ridges silhouetted against an orange sky – and so on. Just recently he'd introduced something quite innovative: a dark pink forest with crystalline flowers at the foot of its trees; this forest filled some of the necessary valleys (well, you had to have valleys if you were going to have mountain ridges to silhouette).

It was relatively straightforward to create such flora in a cyber-world, but could a forest like that actually exist on a planet lit by a red giant? He didn't know; maybe he should base an exobiology project on the question at some point in the future.

While he was musing on this idea, something rather incongruous happened; an owl flew over to him with a letter in its beak. He really would have to do something about the more inappropriate cultural icons he'd been saddled with as defaults in his ownworld!

The letter, which was audiovisual only in a rather muted way, informed him that he'd got a job. His heart sank. He knew that he'd recently been put on the employment register, but he hadn't expected this so soon. And as he read the details of this job he'd been assigned, his heart sank much further.

'What?' he thought, 'This must be the most boring job in the entire universe.' A thought came to him: the reason he'd received this assignment now, so soon after becoming available for work, was that this particular job was THE ONE absolutely no-one wanted to do – it must be. So he declined it, of course.

But it seemed, then, only a matter of seconds before he got a call from someone with a strange name he didn't recognise – the subject line was very succinct – 'Job.' Really just out of curiosity, he took the call. After a cursory greeting, the nondescript avatar which had appeared came straight to the point: 'Please, please just take the job, I can make it worth your while.'

'How?' DeeTee answered, rather incredulously.

'Well,' said the avatar, more uncertainly: 'I... I do have some really cool plugins that'd be great for your ownworld.' And DeeTee was then shown some of these. A few of them were indeed really cool. One was a kind of giant rain; the raindrops were about the size of a house and stayed floating in mid-air. You could jump from one raindrop to another, swimming through each.

'That's great – truly' said DeeTee, 'But, you know, there's so much open source stuff around these days; it's not worth me sacrificing my time just to get hold of that, is it? Sorry, hom – everything worth anything is free now, that's the way it is.' This was indeed the case, and the computing resources of any self-respecting quantum processor were pretty much inexhaustible.

The avatar looked troubled: 'Well, I didn't want to do this, but I can force you to change your mind, believe me. Look, I'm desperate, I've been doing this job for months, and I can't find anyone to take it off me.'

DeeTee thought this was a bit needy and a little threatening, so he terminated the call.

And that was that, DeeTee thought. He'd declined the job; he would be assigned another and then perhaps another until something not too depressingly appalling turned up. DeeTee went on with his life.

For the next few weeks his life consisted mostly of building new things into his ownworld, inviting people over to share it, going over to theirs for parties, etc. And also, he started on some research into exobiology. Additionally, of course, he had to spend some of his time unplugged. This was tiresome but necessary. Obviously, he had to eat and exercise; just staying plugged in and surviving on fluid nutrients all the time was demonstrably not good for you.

One morning, during his first unplug of the day, he noticed that his solid food packages were running low, so when he plugged in again, he put in an order for some more. The system provided him with a great many options, but he just let it choose; after all, there were much better things to savour when you were plugged in. Real food was just fuel.

On the other hand, every machine needs fuel, even a biological, wet-ware machine. And in a few days he ran out of solids, and no driverless van had delivered replacements.

DeeTee selected the feedback option – slightly ironically, he thought; 'Hey!' he said, 'I've had no real-food delivery, what's going on? I'm actually feeling *actually* hungry.'

DeeTee settled himself in for the customary longish irritating pause which was usual when waiting for a response from feedback, but this pause did not materialise. Instead the same avatar who had practically begged him to take that awful job appeared almost immediately – with a slightly more confident expression on its face this time 'OK, I guess you got my message;

so are you going to take the job, or are you going to let yourself starve?'

'What?!' DeeTee was surprised by this sudden re-appearance, somewhat confused, and more than a little shocked by what the avatar had said.

'You read the job description.' said the avatar 'This is the kind of thing I'm in charge of – that's what the job entails – remember? So, yeah, you're right, I'm blackmailing you. If you don't change your mind and take this job; I'll starve you to death.'

'What?!'

'Well, not to death, I'm not going to be as evil as all that – I don't think – but I'll certainly keep you feeling hungry all the time.'

DeeTee digested this – *that* irony was lost on him, perhaps fortunately.

'Look...' said the avatar.

DeeTee peremptorily cut off the call, but in a few days he was weakening, both literally and metaphorically. When the avatar called again, he answered.

'Well?' said the avatar.

'Hey you can't do this!'

'Yes I can – and you know it.'

'I'll complain.'

'The feedback will go to me.'

'You can't do this!' DeeTee repeated, weakly, knowing that this statement was simply untrue. Then he had an idea, 'I'll go to the user's forum; I'll tell them what's happening. You'll get censured.'

'Yeah, perhaps – eventually – not exactly the kind of thing they usually deal with, though, is it? And in the meantime, well maybe those food deliveries are gonna stay stopped.'

'You wouldn't!'

'I'm desperate, hom; even I don't know how far I'll go.' And the avatar did indeed sound desperate, 'Look, I don't want all this trouble any more than you do, but you *gotta* take the job, hom, it's only fair, and look... I... I'll give you my entire ownworld; I'll start again from scratch. I've got aliens, animals, even some sentient – come on, hom.'

DeeTee could hear the desperation in the other's voice. What would he, himself, be driven to in such a situation? He reviewed the other's ownworld and had to admit that the whole thing was pretty good. And it was, really, only fair; someone did have to do the job, and, you know, if people weren't reasonable and didn't compromise then everything would become, well, quite awkward.

'Oh heck, I guess I could do the same as you, get rid of it, when the time comes.'

'Yeah that's right.'

'Alright, alright,' he agreed, knowing that he was going to regret it, but not seeing any sort of reasonable alternative.

'Hey!' DeeTee exclaimed, in sudden realisation, 'Controlling everyone's food supply!'

'And housing and all that' chipped in the other.

'I could get people to do anything!'

'Yeah, but like what? What could you get from them that you can't get for free when you're plugged in anyway? What could you make them do – apart from take on this crummy job, of course.'

'Now you tell me.'

'I know, I know, but thanks, hom.' said the avatar, 'Oh, and there's just one more thing.'

'Oh yeah?' said DeeTee, not anticipating anything good.

'No, No,' said the other, 'it's a perk of the job really.'

'Uh?'

'There's a title that goes with it – didn't you see that?'

'A title?' asked DeeTee, unsure.

'Yeah, like in games when people are called 'Lord' or 'General' or whatever.'

'Oh yeah, I guess, what's the title?'

'President', people are supposed to call you that – 'Mr President' in your case. It's a bit of a tradition – from the past – you know?'

'Oh – great'

'Well, see yaz, Mr President.'

'Yeah' said DeeTee sighing, wondering what he'd done in a past life to end up with this particular short straw.

A narrow escape for the Chelsea Hotel

Robert Ronsson

It was November 1978. Icicles hung from the awning over the entrance of The Hotel Chelsea at 222 West 23rd Street, New York, New York. DJ, as the bustling young property developer was known, hardly noticed the temperature. He was swaddled in a blue cashmere overcoat with a stridently yellow, silk scarf around his neck and he had only been exposed to the chill air for the six strides it took him to cross the sidewalk that separated his limousine from the hotel's double doors.

First-time visitors to the hotel invariably and involuntarily hit an invisible wall within two or three paces of the entrance. Jaws drop. Mouths gape. Dopey, gash smiles split their faces and their eyes widen as a visual storm of paintings and sculpture, the latter often hanging bizarrely from the high ceiling, overwhelms them. DJ, who had never been inside the revered building, was unhindered and unmoved by the explosion of colour and form as he barrelled to the reception desk. The long-haired receptionist, in a white cotton shirt and black trousers, faced the other way.

DJ banged the handily placed bell. 'I have an appointment with Stanley Bard,' he announced.

The receptionist continued to search along the bank of pigeon holes.

DJ frowned. He was not used to being ignored. The thin lips of his wide mouth flattened expressively. 'You, boy! Turn around!'

The 'boy' spun round, presenting DJ with the view of small breasts, possibly bra-less, inside the shirt.

His eyes widened. He couldn't stop a winning smile from spreading across his features like the beam from a lighthouse, despite not being sure whether he was facing a man, a woman or something in between. If she was a woman, which on balance was his assumption, shouldn't she have paid more attention to her complexion, to the texture of her hair? No woman he knew, and he knew a lot of women, would have let herself go like this.

'You want somethin'?' the woman asked.

DJ pulled back his shoulders, leant his head to one side and smiled winningly. 'I already said, I have an appointment with Stanley Bard.'

'That's cool.' She turned back to examine the pigeon holes. Her tight trousers flattered her derriere and DJ, who had the feeling that he had met her somewhere, fought back the urge to shuffle into the confined space behind her. Through gritted teeth, he addressed her back. 'So perhaps you'd like to tell him?'

The woman's shoulders slumped. 'Timur!' she shouted.

An elderly gentleman scuttled round from behind DJ and took up position behind the front desk. He turned to the woman. 'Patti, you shouldn't even be here. I'll tell the others you've been trying to intercept their stashes again.'

'Try it and I'll rip you apart, you old fart" Patti said, but she came round from behind the counter and looked DJ up and down. 'This gentleman has an appointment to see Stan the Man.' She put her hands in her pockets and sauntered towards the rear of the building. DJ watched her swaying profile and regretted not making a move on her.

'Allow me to introduce myself,' Timur said offering DJ his hand.

DJ gave him the death grip.

Timur winced. 'I'm Timur Cimkentli. I'm not the regular bell-hop. I have the job to work off some back rent that I owe Stanley. He's such a fine man, like a huge tree that kids could shelter under in a storm. It is the miracle of this hotel. He would never evict you. You would owe him two months' rent and you would cry to him and he would say, "Don't worry, keep painting, keep painting". Which is fine for a painter but for a photographer who had to sell his camera to buy food ... well, it's not so bad, the work of a bell-hop in The Hotel Chelsea.'

'What did you say your name was again?' How DJ hated that so many Americans had immigrant names.

'Timur Cimkentli, at your service.'

'Mr Cim—,' his mobile lips wrestled with the syllables, 'please take me to Stanley Bard.'

DJ followed the little photographer as, bent forwards as if under an ancient camera's cape, he crossed the lobby and knocked on a nondescript door.

'Who is it?'

'It's Timur!'

'Can you come back later, Timur? I have somebody coming to see me. They're late.'

DJ shook his head and brushed Timur aside. '*I'm* your three-o'clock appointment!' He barged through the door.

A balding man in a crisp white open-necked shirt was seated behind an antique desk. A pair of half-frame glasses hung at chest level on a black, thick-shoelace lanyard. He stood. 'What can I do for you?' he asked.

'It's more what I can do for you. I've come to make you a deal, Mr Bard. I'm going to make The Chelsea Hotel great again.'

'Ah! Mr...'

'Call me DJ.'

'Well, Mr DJ, this is a brave boast. But surely you know that The Chelsea Hotel is not for sale.'

'Not yet.' After removing his overcoat and straightening his tie, DJ breathed deeply, hoping that the puny Stanley Bard would admire and be intimidated by his weightlifter's chest. He pulled a chair up to the desk and sat down, hunching forward and dangling his clasped hands between his spread legs. With his heavy jowls, he looked like a sumo wrestler poised to attack. His red tie hung low almost to his ankles. 'Stanley, let me tell you about the hotel business. I know a lot about the hotel business. Everything anybody needs to know about the hotel business, I know it. Last month Sid Vicious murdered his girlfriend, Nancy Sponging, here—'

'Spungen,' Bard interrupted.

DJ waved it away. 'A detail. She was a beautiful girl – a very beautiful girl.' His mind drifted to the picture he had seen of Nancy in a tight corset. 'Such a terrible loss ... terrible loss. I saw the hotel on TV. The girl's body being carried out of the lobby. The man arrested on the premises. No hotel is going to survive that shit without a major makeover.'

He held up his right hand making an 'O' shape with the forefinger and thumb. 'This could be a top hotel.' His hand thrust forward as if he was launching the points of his argument like darts. 'A classy hotel. A beautiful hotel.' He pursed his lips. 'I've looked at the figures. Even taking into account that these are the tax figures—' he touched a finger to the side of his nose '—you people, you people—' he shook his head theatrically, his smile a flat line across the lower half of his face '—these figures are not good. These are bad figures. Very bad. You have a piece of prime real estate here. These are very bad figures. This hotel has not been performing as it should for years. The return on asset value stinks. Now with this murder...' He shook his head vigorously enough to dislodge the promontory of spun-sugar hair that hung over his forehead. He palmed it back into place and sat back.

Stanley Bard smiled as if he was composing himself to sweet-talk a child, 'Mr DJ, how much do you know about *The Chelsea*?'

DJ waved a hand, 'All I need to know. I've seen the figures.'

'Do you know, for instance, that for a long time it has been a sanctuary for artists, for writers. Mark Twain stayed here—'

No answer.

'You know, the author of *Huckleberry Finn*.'

No answer.

'*Tom Sawyer?*'

No answer.

'Perhaps you'll be familiar with some of our other guests: Dylan Thomas, O Henry, Thomas Wolfe, Leonard Cohen, Janis Joplin ...'

DJ continued shaking his head and looked bemused. If Bard was letting all these people: Mark Twain, Huckleberry Finn, Tom Sawyer, Dylan Thomas stay in the hotel rent-free he'd evict them on day one.

'How about the painters – De Kooning, Jasper Johns, Jackson Pollock?' He pointed at the wall behind DJ.

DJ turned and glanced at the confusion of colour that hung there and shook his head.

Bard sighed. 'How about the playwright Arthur Miller?'

'Wasn't he Marilyn Monroe's husband?'

'Bingo! You may also know Patti Smith. She's here right now. She had a number one record in the summer. *Because the Night?*'

DJ's features had again composed themselves into those of a bemused gorilla before something clicked and he smiled. That's where he'd seen the druggie chick before, she sang that song on *The Midnight Special* television show

As if realising that he would have to do something to regain DJ's attention, Bard cleared his throat and went to the window addressing it as if to lecture the people walking by.

'Some call *The Chelsea* bohemian. I prefer to call it artistic. I created this home for artists over the course of many years, it is a building, a refuge, so respected in the industry, in the cultural community, the artistic community and in the city. I never wanted *The Chelsea* to be conformist. I customised it to its community. So many people wouldn't want this to be disturbed in any way. My tenants like me – tenants liking a landlord, who knew? They respect me and I respect them totally, wholeheartedly. I struggle to think what you could do to improve on the wonderful difference it took me a lifetime to create.'

DJ, who had been shaking his head all through Bard's speech, leant forward. 'You don't get it. Art counts for shit on the bottom line. Your tenants *like* you? What does that mean in dollars? This place is a cess pit. When I came in here I saw the Smith woman trying to score drugs in the reception area—'

Bard's eyes sparkled, 'Dear Patti. What can I say?'

'—the little guy who brought me to your room, Timor Some-immigrant-name, hasn't paid his rent for months. You can't let trash like this get away with it – taking you for a ride. Not if you wanna make this hotel great again.'

'And what would you do?'

'I'd clear out the riff-raff. Banish the dope-pushers. Sack the hangers-on. Clear out the undesirables. Drain the swamp. That's what I'd do, drain the swamp. If I could build a wall, a beautiful wall, to keep out the undesirables, keep out the hangers-on. I'd do it – a high wall.' He put a hand up above his head to indicate that it would be taller even than his 6 foot 4 inches. 'Then once the place was clean with proper guests I'd enforce the rents.'

'You realise that if you did that, you'd destroy everything that makes the hotel what it is. My job is to protect the integrity of *The Chelsea*, to give refuge to this community of friends that, I can see you only regard as strange and kookie.'

'Strange and kookie is a drain on the bottom line!' DJ said. 'Shall I tell you what I see when I look at your hotel? Hookers and tramps trapped here by your strange benevolence, rusted-out plumbing scattering leaks across the landings and the rooms and a sewage system that leaves your guests deprived of sanitation. The crime and hangers-on and drugs that have stolen too many lives and have robbed this place of so much unrealised potential.' His upper body trembled with emotion. 'This American carnage stops right here. I could make it stop right now. I see a beautiful hotel here.'

Bard's eyes twinkled, 'Not without my art. If I sold the hotel to you I would take my art with me.'

DJ laughed. 'The stuff I've seen, you're welcome. This place looks like a yard sale.' He jerked his head back. 'Take the drippy stuff. Take all of it. They're not part of the deal.'

Bard turned back from the window. 'I tell you why I won't sell to you, Mr DJ. It's for the simple reason that I don't think this classic building would be safe in your hands. I have done some homework too. I know that you own the *Bonwit Teller* building on Fifth Avenue and you plan to demolish it to build some sort of Tower – a phallic symbol of your inadequacy.'

DJ made a mental note to look up the word 'fallic'. 'Yeah, maybe you're right,' he said. 'Maybe this place would be better pulled down and a tower, a tall, beautiful tower built here.' He stood up. 'But we're never going to know because you just turned down the best offer you're ever going to get. This was a one-off. I don't come back.'

'Good-bye, Mr DJ,' Bard said, regaining his seat, his eyes still shining as if he was touched by a fever.

On his way through the lobby, DJ scanned the room to see whether Patti Smith was still hanging out there. Timor Thingy was behind the reception counter. DJ's disappointment at the broad's absence lasted for the few steps it took to reach his waiting limousine. He'd console himself with a visit to his latest squeeze who he had recently installed in one of his apartment buildings. Now there was a woman who looked after herself. Admittedly she didn't speak much English but he hadn't chosen her for sparkling conversation.

And as for the glamour of television, if that homely frump he'd met in reception could make it, so could he. It was merely a matter of finding the right show.

That same evening, DJ was slumped on a red-plush banquette that formed one side of a booth in a Tribeca bar. Opposite him a man, who hadn't removed his turned-up-collar trench-coat, nursed a bottle of Stolichnaya Gold vodka. The two men had already downed their welcoming shots and now two glasses stood empty front of them.

The man spoke in a whisper. His fingers nearest the booth's opening rested on his nose so that his cupped palm made the shape of a racehorse's blinker. 'So, tovarishch, the Jew turned you down.'

'He did. But he called it right. I woulda pulled that ugly bitch down and built a tower, another beautiful tower.'

'You must not be in too much hurry, DJ.' His accent mangled the two letters into a four-syllable word. 'We have all time in world.'

DJ's shoulders still slumped. 'I don't like losing. We shoulda had a deal. There were so many weaknesses on his side.'

The man filled the two shot glasses and slid one across the table. 'Drink up. We toast future – budushcheye.'

'Budushcheye!' They both downed the spirit in one.

'Perhaps we learn lesson,' said the man. 'From now when you go into deal we do ground work for you. You go forward with dossier in hand. Even, we soften things up a little for you. How this sound?'

'Good! It sounds good.'

'We can go back for Chelsea Hotel, if you really want it. Make Jew offer he can't refuse.' His shoulders shook. This together with his mirthless smile signified he had made a joke.

DJ shook his head. 'Thanks, but no thanks. Not this time. That deal is dead.'

The man's whisper became quieter still and DJ had to lean forward to hear what he was saying. 'I don't think you know, DJ, how much resource I have at my disposal. You do know, don't you, what your ambition might be, where you want life to go, as big as you want, I can do this for you?'

DJ squared up his shoulders and his chest filled his suit jacket. His voice broke with emotion. 'I know this, tovarishch, and I'll always be grateful.'

'We should own the stars':

Postcapitalism, Techno-Utopianism,

and Blade Runner 2049

Sean Seeger

I

The last few years have seen an explosion of writing on the topic of how impending developments in science and technology are set to radically transform society in the near future. Some of the books in this vein associate these changes with a broader phenomenon they call postcapitalism. Rather than designating a specific type of economic regime, postcapitalism has become a catch-all term for a broad spectrum of attempts to envisage an alternative social order. Writing in this area is necessarily highly speculative, moving freely between sober empirical analysis of current trends and freewheeling flights of imagination about the possibilities of emerging technologies.

So far, postcapitalism has tended to be envisaged from a radical left perspective. For Nick Srnicek and Alex Williams in their book

Inventing the Future (2015), postcapitalism holds out the promise of a post-scarcity, post-work society in which a combination of mass automation, renewable energy, artificial intelligence, and universal basic income facilitate the transition to a high-tech egalitarian utopia. If a new generation of robots can be relied on to produce everything humanity needs, Srnicek and Williams contend, then, as long as the robots are collectively owned and directed, the groundwork will have been laid for a society not unlike the classless civilisation depicted in *Star Trek*, in which material want has been abolished. The logic of this position was succinctly formulated by the physicist Stephen Hawking in a copiously re-tweeted remark made in an interview in 2016: 'Everyone can enjoy a life of luxurious leisure if the machine-produced wealth is shared, or most people can end up miserably poor if the machine owners successfully lobby against wealth redistribution.'

A similar line of thought animates Paul Mason's book *Postcapitalism: A Guide to Our Future* (2015), as well as providing the impetus for the journalist Aaron Bastani's repeated calls for what he has termed 'fully automated luxury communism'. Meanwhile, Rutger Bregman's bestselling *Utopia for Realists* (2017), whilst somewhat more pragmatic in its orientation, nevertheless envisages a reorganisation of social life no less thoroughgoing than that sketched by his more radical postcapitalist fellow travellers.

At the same time, albeit from an opposing political perspective, equally ambitious claims on behalf of technology's ability to remake society over the coming decades have been advanced by some of the most influential figures in the contemporary tech world, as detailed in Noam Cohen's important book *The Know-It-Alls* (2017). As Cohen and others have argued, this new global elite – a mixture of entrepreneurs, software designers, biotech investors, futurists, libertarian ideologues, and self-proclaimed visionaries – has begun to coalesce into a form of technocracy which threatens to undermine democratic politics. Names typically associated with this trend include Peter Thiel (of PayPal fame), Marc Andreessen (a key figure in the early development of the internet), Larry Page and Sergey Brin (of Google), Ray Kurzweil (now also at Google), Bill Gates (Microsoft), Jeff Bezos (Amazon), Reid Hoffman (LinkedIn), Mark Zuckerberg (Facebook), and, from beyond Silicon Valley, Elon Musk (Tesla and SpaceX). Of these, Thiel, Kurtzweil, and Musk have been the most notable for their sweeping pronouncements on the technological destiny of humanity, whether in the form of immortality (Thiel), self-aware machines (Kurtzweil), or space colonisation (Musk).

More recently still, a number of sceptical voices have emerged in the debates around technological change in the present century. Whereas commentators like Srnicek and Williams see the new technologies as liberating human beings from material scarcity, these more pessimistic critics see in the same technologies the potential for an unparalleled extension of the apparatus of social control, and even, in some cases, the vanishing of the human altogether.

In very different registers and from very different points of view, Peter Frase's *Four Futures* (2016), Adam Greenfield's *Radical Technologies* (2017), Jonathan Taplin's *Move Fast and Break Things* (2017), and Mark O'Connell's *To Be a Machine* (2017) – to take just four representative examples – all foresee profound threats arising from technology in the near future. For Frase, while mass automation could be made to serve progressive ends, it could just as easily give rise to the nightmarish scenario he dubs 'exterminism' – a neo-feudal order in which the elite, having monopolised the new machines, retreats into fortified enclaves, leaving the majority to fend for themselves in an ecologically devastated world. Unlike some other commentators on the radical left, Frase sees the projected wave of new developments as decidedly ambiguous in nature: technology simultaneously promises to fulfil the aims of *The Communist Manifesto* while at the same time threatening to exacerbate and permanently entrench existing inequalities.

Greenfield and Taplin, meanwhile, are concerned with the social and political influence of the latest digital technologies, which they see as paving the way for technocracy – an anti-democratic ideology that first arose in the 1930s but which is rapidly becoming the dominant worldview of today's tech elite. As Roger Luckhurst observes, 'Advocates of technocratic solutions transcended the politically riven landscape of the 1930s: above capitalism, communism, or fascism, they simply promised to run the machine more efficiently.' In the same way, under the cover of 'neutral' efficiency calculations, 'unbiased' algorithms, and the rhetoric of 'irresistible' technological progress, the latest generation of technocrats is increasingly turning against what it sees as outmoded systems of government, taxation, antitrust legislation, and state control.

Lastly, in *To Be a Machine*, Mark O'Connell interviews prominent members of the international transhumanist movement, for whom the human mind and body are themselves obsolete technologies which ought to be retired and replaced – a belief which, as O'Connell discovered during the course of his research, was 'for all its apparent extremity and strangeness... nonetheless exerting certain formative pressures on the culture of Silicon Valley, and thereby the broader cultural imagination of technology [today].' As Yuval Noah Harari has recently argued in *Homo Deus: A Brief History of Tomorrow* (2017), a suggestive study of long-term technological trends, such an outlook, wedded to a programme of self-directed human evolution, has the potential to initiate a new chapter in the history of life on earth, one in which biology has been transcended and mind subsists on a wholly synthetic platform.

For anyone familiar with the science fiction, speculative fiction, utopian, and dystopian literary traditions of the nineteenth and twentieth centuries, few of the technologies making headlines today will seem especially novel. Robots, self-driving vehicles, autonomous drones, artificial superintelligence, synthetic biology, radical life extension, whole brain emulation, mind uploading, cryopreservation, wetware, biohacking, gene editing, nanotechnology, geoengineering, terraforming – none of these is a wholly new concept, even if their implementation had been largely confined to the fictional domain until now. Virtually all of them have been addressed, at one time or another, by writers and filmmakers interested in imagining the future, and in what such imagining might tell us about the present.

Literature and cinema in the twenty-first century continue to provide a fruitful space in which to think through some of the issues raised by the prospect of disruptive technological change. One particularly rich and suggestive example here is Denis Villeneuve's film *Blade Runner 2049*, which engages with some of the most pressing concerns raised by authors like Cohen, Frase, Greenfield, Taplin, O'Connell, and others who have come to harbour deep misgivings about the techno-utopianism present in contemporary culture.

II

Blade Runner 2049 is a dark, brooding science fiction film released in 2017. It is a sequel to Ridley Scott's *Blade Runner* (1982), itself a loose adaptation of Philip K Dick's cult dystopian novel *Do Androids Dream of Electric Sheep?* (1968). In the first *Blade Runner* film, a group called the Tyrell Corporation has created a race of artificial beings virtually indistinguishable from humans known as Replicants. The Replicants are designed to have superhuman strength and are used as disposable slave labour on off-world colonies. As intelligent, self-aware creatures, however, Replicants sometimes refuse to fulfil the roles assigned to them, openly rebelling against their human masters.

Blade Runner 2049 is set thirty years after the events depicted in Scott's original film. During the intervening period, a global ecological collapse has occurred, ushering in an age of extreme scarcity. As the film's opening text informs us, 'this has led to the rise of the industrialist Niander Wallace, whose mastery of synthetic farming averted famine.' The Tyrell Corporation has meanwhile been bankrupted as a result of a prohibition on Replicant manufacture in response to a series of violent uprisings in the colonies. Wallace has since taken over the remnants of the corporation and put Replicants back into production after devising a new model designed to be more compliant than its forerunners.

A first thing to note about *Blade Runner 2049* is that, like every major dystopia, the film is on one level an exercise in worldbuilding, meaning that the world in which the action takes place reveals as much about this version of the future as the action itself – indeed, arguably more so. Evidence of the fate of the natural world, for instance, is apparent throughout. Almost all plant and animal life has been extinguished. All food is synthesised and food production takes place exclusively in facilities owned by the Wallace Corporation. Water is strictly rationed: when the protagonist takes a shower, he is blasted with high pressure water for just two seconds while an electronic voice announces, '99.9% detoxified water'. Likewise, whilst in *Blade Runner* East Asian characters and languages had been highly visible, in the sequel we also hear citizens speaking a range of

Eastern European and African languages, suggesting that mass migration has accelerated in response to global crises.

Los Angeles, the only urban settlement we see, is a looming, overcrowded city bordered to the west by gigantic sea defences built to protect against rising sea levels, and to the north by immense stretches of waste dumping ground. When we first see it, the cityscape itself is an undifferentiated smear of angular shapes half glimpsed in brief bursts of light against the pitch-black night sky. When day comes, the sun is scarcely visible and the air outside is thick with pollution. All of this is reflected in the musical theme associated with these sequences: an oppressive wall of sound carried along by an implacable, rapid drum beat and punctuated at points by agitated electronic sounds which rise and fall in jagged waves like distant alarm signals. Whatever astonishing technological advances have been made in this scenario, they have clearly not been harnessed for the sake of the maintenance of the environment or the preservation of the earth.

A second key element of this dystopia worth commenting on is the decidedly marginal role played in it by human beings. Whereas the first *Blade Runner* film had made much of the blurring of the boundary between human and Replicant, in the sequel this ambiguity is for the most part eliminated. In the first scene of the film, set on a Wallace protein farm outside the city limits, the protagonist, known simply as K (played by Ryan Gosling), is clearly identified as a Replicant from the outset. This point is made quite emphatically when we see K repeatedly pummelled against a wall by another Replicant until he is seen bursting out the other side amidst a heap of debris in a way which would almost certainly have been fatal for a human being. K's pain threshold is also exceptionally high: he scarcely reacts when a knife is thrust into his side during the same sequence. In this way, we are made viscerally aware that we are following someone who is not human.

When K returns to his flat – a cramped, cell-like living unit in a poorly maintained apartment building – we are given an insight into his domestic life. After he has settled, a female voice from off-screen which we assume to belong to his partner tells K that she is putting the finishing touches to his evening meal: 'I'm trying a new recipe. I think you'll like it.' Neither the woman nor the meal materialises, however – at least, not in the form we had anticipated. K's partner, Joi (played by Ana de Armas) is revealed to be a holographic simulation, beamed into the room by a projector which traverses the ceiling of the living area. The meal which is put in front of K – a juicy steak and selection of fresh vegetables – is likewise a mere image positioned so as to cover up the meal K has previously prepared himself: a bowl containing a decidedly unappetising, presumably vitamin-enriched foam-like substance.

Joi is a software application designed to serve as a romantic companion. Like the commercially available sex robots recently criticised by numerous feminist commentators, Joi is unfailingly acquiescent and eager to please. Throughout this scene, she is constantly assessing K's mood, spontaneously changing her clothes and hairstyle from one moment to the next to better match it. When K looks uninterested, Joi asks him to read to her but he declines. Undeterred, she throws the book aside, changes her dress and hairstyle once again, and asks him to dance. At one point, while receiving an upgrade, Joi's 'stats' appear in the air beside her: her height, body type, face type, skin tone, eye colour, lip colour, hair colour, hair style, ethnicity, and language are all customisable like the options on any other digital device. Later in the film, hyper-sexualised advertisements for the Joi model hologram can be seen being projected beside overhead walkways and on the sides of buildings. 'Joi can be anything you want her to be', one slogan informs us.

The sequence in K's flat is notable for the lack of a human presence: it depicts, after all, the interaction of a machine – valued for its superhuman strength and resilience – with a piece of software – valued for its tireless, permanent availability. As such, the sequence may be read as both an unsettling depiction of a post-human condition – in which human limitations are overcome at the cost of the obsolescence of the human – and a warning about the tendency of technology to reproduce existing power relations – in this case of a starkly gendered nature.

III

Blade Runner 2049's main cast of characters in fact contains strikingly few human beings: with the exception of K's boss – who, tellingly, dies at the hands of a Replicant – the only human being with a significant role in the plot is Niander Wallace himself (played by Jared Leto). Before we are first introduced to Wallace, on-screen text announces the scene's location: 'Wallace Corporation. Earth headquarters.' There is an ambiguity in this wording which is left open: is this the headquarters of the corporation or the headquarters of earth? Such is the influence of Wallace over every aspect of life in 2049, it would seem reasonable to assume the latter.

Shot from a low angle so as to emphasise their extraordinary height, the three great Wallace Towers dwarf the pyramid buildings of the Tyrell Corporation from the first *Blade Runner*. By comparison with the sleek, ultra-corporate styling of the Wallace Towers, Tyrell's architectural preferences strike us as an exercise in nostalgia, with their eccentric, pseudo-Egyptian styling appearing almost quaint beside the thrusting, slab-like forms which have supplanted them. This striking visual contrast is combined with a cascade of deep and resonant choral voices on the soundtrack, heightening the sense of immensity and even sublimity which the Towers exude.

During his first on-screen appearance, Wallace outlines his Promethean ambitions before lamenting a major barrier his work has come up against. Tyrell, we learn, had managed to create Replicants which were able to give birth, but the means to do this was lost in the chaos of the following decades. In a remarkable speech which alludes to both Milton's *Paradise Lost* and some of the more ambitious designs of the tech billionaire Elon Musk, Wallace at one point speaks contemptuously of his own pioneering role in colonising nine planets: 'I brought back the Angels and took us to nine new worlds. Nine. A child can count to nine on fingers. We should own the stars.' Building to a crescendo, he exclaims, 'More. Worlds beyond worlds, diamond shores. We could storm Eden and retake her.'

In stark contrast to all this, another sequence of the film depicts life amidst Los Angeles' waste dumping grounds. These are inhabited by assorted outcasts and desperate criminal gangs among others. In one scene, hundreds of orphaned children are shown labouring in a cavernous workhouse built under a toppled satellite dish, where they are tasked with stripping down old technology for spare parts. As their brutal overseer remarks to K at one point, collecting nickel for spaceships is the closest anyone on earth will get to 'the grand life off-world.'

In the post-human future over which Wallace presides, the widespread obsolescence of human beings projected by techno-utopianism has been largely realised, though with none of the liberatory effects anticipated by its more enthusiastic exponents. Unprecedented progress in the colonisation of other planets has also been made, but there is no indication that these developments have benefited anyone on earth, which has been consigned to near-ruin while the new elite push out into the cosmos. Space exploration – the storming of Eden – has generated inconceivable wealth, yet a just and equitable way of life seems further away than ever, with neo-Dickensian conditions proliferating on the margins of society and alienation and deprivation the norm for the majority. The divorce between technological and social progress is virtually complete.

*

Of the two possible futures which he envisaged in 2016, the one utopian and the other dystopian, Stephen Hawking noted that, 'So far, the trend seems to be toward the second option, with technology driving ever-increasing inequality.' *Blade Runner 2049* imagines what a world in which this trend has been allowed to continue might look like. As such, it may be read in a line of dystopias from E M Forster's *The Machine Stops* and Aldous Huxley's *Brave New World* to Margaret Atwood's *The Handmaid's Tale* and Octavia Butler's *Parable of the Sower*, in each of which the resources of fiction are employed to scrutinise tendencies within the author's own historical moment. *Blade Runner 2049* depicts a future in which at least some of the predictions of today's techno-utopians have come true. One question the film leaves us with is that of how the coming technologies might be made to enrich human life and serve collective social ends as opposed to intensifying existing patterns of inequality, exploitation, and ecological devastation.

Tempest on Tyneside

Justine Sless

'There'll be boatloads of them tonight Joe,' I say as we sup on a pint, looking out over Roker Beach, 'hundreds of them, thirsty and gagging to see a match.'

'I never bother going, now man, it's just too hard to get to the stadium because of all the storm work. I just can't get there.' Joe belches, taps his pint glass, signals to the barman for another. 'Daft buggers, coming up here for the drink and the footy every weekend. Who'd do the journey on a night like this an' all? I said to the missus this morning, it's like being back in the glory days but it's not steel, ships or coal that's putting us on the map, now like.'

'Listen to this man,' I read the update from *The Echo* that's pulsing across my data screen, '*All working men's clubs are to be reopened to help cope with the influx of beer drinkers from the south.* Why man, we just need a comedian like The Little Waster and the clubs would be more popular than the footy. H'way, let's get down to the pier.'

'Hey up Dave, here's trouble,' Joe nods towards the window overlooking the sea as he swallows the last of his pint. The lighthouse beacon is flashing blue. A boat with a huge dent in the hull is being pulled in by two trawlermen. Waves are hurtling over the forty-foot embankments, and chunks of rocks and debris shoot up like they have been pelted from a catapult. Some of them land on the pathway to the marina, others disappear back into the blackness of the water.

Along the esplanade, stallholders pause and look up from stringing lanterns and setting up fish bars and beer tents. The blue light flickers for a moment more, then changes back to white. With the boat safely berthed, the stallholders return to their tasks.

We wave to the gadgee on a ladder as we head over to see if it's the boat we've been waiting for. I nudge Joe. 'I don't know why they bother changing those signs. This global monarchy malarkey isn't working out. Whose turn is it now anyway? Last time I looked it was Prospero of Poland's go, wasn't it? He must have been shot.'

The gadgee pulls down the old sign and replaces it with a new yellow triangle proclaiming *October 2026 Monarchy, Sebastian of Denmark*.

By the time we get down to the marina, two trawlermen are guiding the boat into its moorings. It takes all their strength to pull it in from the sea, which is rearing up and charging at the marina like an untamed beast. The small vessel lifts for a moment and they almost lose it. As it descends, they throw buoys around it to buffer the impact of the swell.

A lass crawls out from the cabin and the trawlermen shout in unison the salutation of welcome reserved for women of her kind: '*Alreet pettle!*' She's wearing tight black jeans, a heavy woollen overcoat, twelve-hole maroon doc martens, and sports a bright blue mohawk that's spiky despite the driving rain.

'My name's Miranda,' she says to the trawlermen. 'I've got to get to my allocated town quickly. I'll need some scran, a pushbike or whatever youse lot are using to get around. We've lost loads of time getting back here from south of the Wear.

A burly bloke with a mask of tattoos covering his face and bald head emerges from the cabin. As he attempts to disembark from the boat, the trawlermen, as a precaution, hold him down.

'Let me go, you bloody dickheads!' The burly bloke yells at them. 'We've been on that boat for days trying to land between the storms. I'm from around here. I'm not here to steal the beer for god's sake.'

The trawlermen loosen their grip, murmur an apology and head off down the marina to prepare for the arrival of the boats carrying the Southerners.

'Alreet pettle?' I proffer my hand to Miranda. 'I'm Dave and this is Joe. We're townmen, we'll get you sorted in no time. Have you Divined where you've got to go yet?'

'Yes, I've got to get to South Shields,' Miranda replies, holding out her arms to interpret the storm.

'Righto then pet, let's get going once you've done your Divining,' I say. 'You've got a right job ahead of you at the Tyne mind. I've not been up there but I've heard that the bridges are down, and the Geordies are well pissed off about having to come by boat instead of by road for their beer.'

Miranda looks along the length of her outstretched arms. Her fingers are spread wide apart and her body tenses so much that I look out to the churning great North Sea to try and understand what she can sense. But all I can glean is that the sea looks like there's a mad man under it and he's having a fit. There's men that say after a few pints they can Divine, but they are full of shite and the last time someone believed one of them, there were lives and towns lost.

'We need to go now,' Miranda says, lowering her arms. 'We'll need the light from the stadium to guide us for what's coming.' She cracks her neck from side to side in readiness for the work ahead of her. The burly bloke is surveying the damage to the hull of the boat. She thanks him for bringing her ashore and we head up to the market area which is beginning to fill with punters.

'Here, get this down yer neck pet,' I hand her a steaming bit of battered cod, a pile of chips and a pint from The Fish Tent. 'On the house,' the stallholder says. 'Joe tells me you're a Tempestian, pet. It's a bloody awful night and I wouldn't want to Divine where the storm will land next.'

'Thanks,' Miranda says through a mouthful of food. We scoff the scran, sink the pints and head to the bike shed.

'Oh hell, look at this will you?' My data screen is pinging with news updates. 'Down south, Lizard Point, Dover and Portsmouth are gone and up north the waters have sunk Inverness.' Joe shakes his head and says, 'It's the single malt I can't help thinking about, all of those distilleries gone forever. It's just criminal.'

The blare of a foghorn makes us all turn around. 'Hey up, the posh gits have arrived,' Joe says.

A flotilla of huge vessels jostle and jump like they are on a bouncy castle before coming to a stop at the end of the pier. Several of the trawlermen link arms to make sure they don't get blown away as they wait for the passengers to disembark. Predictably, the Southerners act like the waves and the pissing rain are an insult and try to brush off the water and bits of debris that land on them as they make their way to the night market.

Some of them are wearing rain ponchos with *Sunderland's famous footy and beer tours* printed on them, others are wearing tweed jackets that are already soaked through. The wind is so strong that the passengers make their way along the pier clinging to each other and to the mooring ropes, so they don't get blown away.

'We've got to go now,' Miranda says, agitated by the gathering storm. We get on the bikes, put up the wind sails and head to South Shields. As we head out of Roker towards the Stadium of Light, we see the gadgee returning with a new monarchy sign. 'Seriously why does he even bother? No sooner has he put the sign up than the news changes and another reign begins,' I say as I begin to pedal.

The wind catches the bikes' sails and it takes us no time at all to ride the two miles to the Stadium of Light. The floodlights are blazing in readiness for the game and the brightness radiates for miles. The windmills around the outside of the stadium are whizzing and the pong of hops from the Vaux brewery next door is so strong that I almost choke on it.

Miranda gets off her bike so she can Divine close to the lights. She genuflects in front of the statue of Elsie the Housewife and holds out her arms once more.

'I can hear it.' Miranda's voice is deep and scary.

'Hear what pet?' I ask, not really wanting to know the answer.

'The fault line, it's moving.'

Joe is filling up his glass at the turnstile for the second time.

'Joe finish yer beer man, we need to get going,' I yell at him.

'It's all right,' says Miranda. 'We've all got time for a quick pint. We'll need it.'

As we drink down the beers, the team arrives for the night's match. Maureen, the team captain, waves at us as they file past through the turnstiles. We hold up our pint glasses by way of a salute.

'Good luck lasses, all the best for the game,' I say shyly, not quite believing that the whole of the Sunderland team, now top in the World League, have just walked past me.

'H'way lads, let's get up to the Tyne, afore the roads clog up with footy crowds,' Miranda shouts to us above the wind that sounds like a siren's wail. The bike's windsails flap and bend in the wind, and we have to hold on tight to the handlebars as we make our way through Cleadon.

At the ancient White Horse painting, Miranda commands us to stop. 'This,' she says pointing to the stone surrounding the painting, 'is magnesium limestone, from the Permian Age. It runs from South Shields to Sunderland and beyond to the edge of the North Yorkshire Moors, dating back to a time when the world was at its most stable point in history. And this small deposit running from the mouth of the Tyne to the mouth of the Wear, this rock is what will save us.'

Her hands clasp and unclasp and her face, lit intermittently by the passing beam from the stadium, is calm and radiant. Her eyebrows are dark against her alabaster skin. I'm tempted to ask her how often she needs to pluck them to keep their lovely shape.

'The waves we've been getting and this wind,' she's shouting now, above the screech of the wind, 'is from the carbon sequestration that they tried to do on the oil rigs back in the eighties. They tried to capture carbon and store it in a reservoir, the dickheads. Now there are just bloody great sink holes in the ocean and that is what's causing the storms. H'way, I'll know more when we get to South Shields.'

We head up the road just as people start coming out of their houses to make their way to the match. They've all got their footy scarves, hats and jumpers on.

As we get closer to South Shields there are hundreds of people on bikes with their sails pointed north, heading to the footy. There are mams with bairns strapped to their backs and girls with pictures of their favourite players printed on their bike sails. Some have tried to get all sixteen team members on and they crowd together – Masie Duncan, Laura Davis, Debbie Moore, and all the others – in their Sunderland tops, smiling out to the wind.

Beams of light from the stadium move over the sea where houses, cars and trees are being tossed around like balls in a bingo cage. It gets harder to move through the oncoming footy traffic and stay stable in the wind. I can hear my screen pinging but don't dare stop to see what the storms are up to now. The rain is lashing down so hard it feels like even my eye sockets are filled with it. My legs are getting heavier with the wet. I can see that Joe is struggling and hope he doesn't insist on stopping at the next beer tap. Miranda looks back at us to check if we're keeping up. Her blue mohawk is flattened now, like the wing of a bird. The sky has turned from dense black to a deep purple, the moon is nowhere to be seen and the wind changes pitch, howling like an animal in distress.

People are swarming out of their houses, looking up at the sky, fastening their jackets and seeming determined, no matter what, to make it to the night's game. At various points, they lean against beer taps, scull pints and chat. As I ride past, I catch snatches of conversation.

'Oh aye, this is a strong wind, this one mind.'

'Sunderland's going to win, last match of the season, they can't lose.'

'I hear there's a new kind of potato being grown that can withstand floodwaters.'

As we reach the mouth of the Tyne, a massive piece of debris hurled into the air from a wave lands in front of us. Miranda swerves on her bike to avoid it, jumps off to get a closer look and yells at us, 'Have a look at this lads, it's a bit of Buckingham Palace.' She laughs and touches the twisted metal sign hanging from the sandstone balustrade with the words *Tours of Buckingham Palace start here*, only just legible from the battering it has received from the sea.

I've seen storms rage for years now and always think that it can get no worse, that there cannot be any more lives lost, that the bloated animal carcasses and human bodies washed up on the beach next to the amusement park has to stop at some point. But this bit of Buckingham Palace landing in the mouth of the River Tyne sends a shiver down me, like I've just had to eat raw black pudding with not a drop of beer to swill it down.

I don't need to look at my screen for an update. I know that the storm has taken London and if the debris can get this far, this fast, then all the sandbags in the world can't save us.

Miranda doesn't look the least bit despondent though. She holds open her arms and flings her head back, like a replica Angel of the North.

'The limestone!' She's laughing, her mouth is open and her hands quiver as she divines the storm: 'The limestone starts here at the mouth of the Tyne and continues over to Blaydon, down to Durham and across to Consett, then radiates to North Yorkshire.'

Joe's gone white. The wind is so strong now that there is a sheer wall of water at the mouth of the river. Miranda is holding up her hands to the water wall and screaming, 'Magnesian limestone is composed of carbonate of lime and carbonate of magnesia in variable proportions. Here lies silica, iron and alumina,' she roars into the howling wind. Her chest is heaving with the exertion. I could murder a pint but now, probably, wouldn't be a good time. Around us there is rubble: cars twisted like flannels that have been squeezed out, road signs, strips of metal, tree trunks piled upon fridges and oil drums.

Above the roar of it all, we hear the wail of the siren from the Stadium of Light as the game kicks off, followed by a huge cheer from the crowd. And in that same moment the wall of water drops as if defeated and retreats along the estuary of the river to the sea, leaving in its wake a devastated landscape.

'The magnesium limestone,' Miranda tells us, breathless, 'that's what has saved us. From the mouth of the Tyne to the mouth of the Wear, the sea cannot attack this rock formation. It's impenetrable. And this,' she says, her arms outstretched, her fingers rigid, 'this piece of land covered in limestone stretching for sixty-five miles, this is all there is left. This is England.'

On Boredom Isle

Elisa Marcella Webb

The sea like the wind was all around us

We didn't go up for Christmas, too cold, too fucking far, Pa said. But this year we were going. The train rattled over the bridge, across the bay. I hoped to see snow. I hoped to see frozen ocean. I was disappointed. Glad I didn't mention it to Pa and Ma. They would just laugh: you'll be expecting polar bears next.

It wasn't cold, just very windy. We stepped off at the small station, someone's house really. Their washing slapped in the breeze, cheap T-shirts and ratty pillow cases.

'We'll walk,' said Pa, adjusting his rucksack, passing me mine. We always walked, even when we had suitcases. It wasn't that there weren't trucks on the island; people just didn't use them when they could walk.

We braced ourselves against the wind, the air smelled of salty seaweed. Gulls wheeled overhead. It was fierce along the causeway. The sky grey, the sea even greyer, choppy round the edges. No good expecting a Christmas tree. Molly Lucas didn't hold with trees. I wondered if we'd live on porridge and toast.

'Jesus, Mary and Joseph,' said Ma. 'If we didn't take tins we'd die of the scurvy'. Tins clanked as she jumped down from the stile.

Molly Lucas appeared up on the bluff, holding her apron against the wind. The dog, Pot, ran towards us, bald patches in his black fur. He jumped about nipping. Pa kicked out: 'Gerr out of it'. Pot retreated, pretending he was interested in a sheep's skull, nestling in the long grass. The kitchen was warm only because Molly Lucas shut out the wind.

'I'll put the kettle on,' said Molly Lucas, running the tap full blast. Water thundered into the enamel kettle.

'You're to go up and drop your things, same room as always,' she laughed at her old joke.

I banged up the stairs in protest. Pot jumped ahead. Then he tried to double back, so he could nip me from behind. Poor bugger, the boredom had done him in. Welcome to Boredom Isle. I dumped my rucksack by the bed. Pot growled and ran towards it, hoping it was alive. He lay down and began to chew the straps. He smelt like bad breath. I sat on the hard bed, the faded eiderdown slithering under my jeans. The window gazed out to sea; even the room wanted to escape.

Later I went down for tea. The house smelt of Wrights' Coal Tar soap. There was toast and very brown tea, steaming in mugs. There were some pink biscuits on a chipped green plate. Ma sat holding a mug for ballast. Pa stood with his back to the range. Molly Lucas stopped talking and stared at me.

'It's okay, Molly Lucas,' said Ma. 'We've been open about... your sister who's dying. We're very sad... you've a dying sister'. She spoke as if she was reading a note.

'Well,' said Molly Lucas, pushing the butter dish towards me.

'She's dying up there now. Dying, though she may come down for a hot chocolate.'

Molly Lucas glanced at Ma with raised eyebrows. Ma sucked air through her teeth. I had no idea hot chocolate was on offer.

The next few days I spent wandering the bluff staring out to sea. I used to hope a ferry would hit the rocks. This would give us all something to do. We could run about shouting. I would call the Coastguard, Ma the emergency services. Then Pa and I would drag people from the sea, rescue flotsam and jetsam, whatever that was. I wouldn't be able to save a cat trapped in its basket. Shame. They'd spent cash at the vets getting it fixed, typical outlanders... But nothing ever happened. I poked at rock pools and pushed my boots into dark sand. The sea was miles and miles away. The beach was so wide it made me tired just to think about it.

On Christmas Day I saw her. The Dying Sister. She was heading towards me. I stopped poking limpets. She didn't look as if she was dying; she was thin, but not skeletal. Skeletal: a good word, a beach word. Later I wrote it in the sand in giant letters. S K E L E T A L.

'Hello,' she called. She held out her hand. My hand was gritty. Her hand was cool and fine. Her hair whipped about her face. She shivered in her black sweater and folded her arms.

'Shall we walk?' she said. So we did. We walked for ages that first time. She hummed and picked up small pink shells. She kept some. I did the same. I found a yellow spiral and a black pebble with a white vein.

Pot bounded over to join us. I wanted to shout fuck off, away with your nonsense. But she picked up a stick, threw it as far from us as possible. When the dog came back, all hysterical slobber, I threw the stick even further. She laughed, 'He'll burst'. Then she yawned. 'Enough. I'm back to bed. Tiring.' Or did she say dying? The wind had burned my ears. Pot was back rubbing his head down my legs. I rubbed his head. When I looked up she was away by the bluff.

The last time I saw her, I almost didn't. There had been a storm overnight. The beach was strewn with seaweed, tangled red nets, and rusty beer cans. I caught the smell of cigarette smoke. She was sitting on the rocks, just below the house. She frowned and offered me a fag. Like a big fool I shook my head. She was watching four men struggling down the crumbling steps. A peeling dinghy rocked in the surf. They were carrying a long box, like an outsized suitcase. She laughed. One of the men slipped and stumbled; the box slid forward and hit the heavy sand. I didn't understand. The box dropper swore. Then glanced over, nodding. The men stopped, then with a tired effort wrenched the box free and slapped their way across the rills. I sat down. Pot sat next to me. I rubbed his back. She drew on the fag, blowing out smoke. The wind whistled through the dry grass, cutting into my kidneys. The men shoved the box into the boat and pushed off onto the sea. She waved. The man who had dropped the box saluted.

'I want to go by sea, not down the causeway... They're practising...' she snorted. 'Trust Molly Lucas'. She stubbed her fag out on the rock and flicked it into the air. It landed in a small puddle, floating like an exclamation mark on the freckled beach.

And the sea was all around us

Afterword

Tempest is our third anthology. The first was *Refugees and Peacekeepers,* published in 2017 and the second was *My Europe,* published in 2018. The anthologies attempt to address contemporary political themes in thought-provoking ways.

As yet, there are no real solutions for the appalling situation of many refugees. People and institutions such as the EU remain apathetic about their plight. Various countries are still experiencing violent conflict. We are confused by climate change denial, anti-gun-control, flagrant arms-dealing and its effect on world peace. This general instability – all in the name of fast-buck capitalism and the uncertainty about the future of the EU and Brexit – is concerning, to say the least. The surge in toxic right-wing populist and extremist movements continues. Shockingly, Brazil is the latest country which has succumbed to a would-be dictatorship.

And Trump is seeking re-election in 2020. As I write, the House of Representatives is no longer under Republican control, but the President has difficulty with the truth and his radical and divisive agenda is focusing on the negative, hopelessness and despair.

But why are he and others so popular? Is it because of a sense of powerlessness and frustration felt by many of the electorate and incited by the media? It has become fashionable to allow populists in Europe and elsewhere to spout hatred, intolerance, racism, sexism and xenophobia. All this, while the rest of us feel fearful and anxious about our democratic rights.

As Gary Younge said, "...there is potency in this powerlessness. With sufficient encouragement, the rage it creates – the frustration it engenders, the nostalgia it spawns – can have a disruptive and corrosive impact on politics."

We must try to overcome our resentment and disappointment in these tempestuous political times and continue the fight for a better future. It is our responsibility to strive for a more democratic, tolerant and fair society.

Patricia Borlenghi

Publisher

Acknowledgements

Thanks to Janette Turner Hospital for kind permission to use the quote from *The Magician*.

Thanks to Steven Pinker who was 'honoured' to allow the quote from his interview published in The Guardian, 11 February 2018.

Permission to use the quote from *The Nix* by Nathan Hill was granted by Pan Macmillan (16 March 2018).

Thanks to George Monbiot for kind permission to quote from his article published in The Guardian, 19 July 2017.

Thanks to Barbara Taylor for kind permission to quote from her article published in The Guardian, 25 February 2017.

Thanks to Patrick Wright for kind permission to reproduce his New Statesman article, published 17 June 1988.

Thanks to Ivana Bartoletti for kind permission to reproduce her article, 'Women must act now, or male-designed robots will take over our lives', first published in The Guardian, 13 March 2018.

Thanks to Chantal Mouffe for kind permission to reproduce her article, 'Populists are on the rise but this can be a moment for progressives too' first published in The Guardian, 10 September 2018.

Thanks to Gary Younge for kind permission to quote from his article published in The Guardian, 6 July 2018.

Editors

Anna Vaught is a novelist, essayist, poet, editor, proofreader, reviewer and also a secondary English teacher, tutor, mentor to young people, mental health campaigner and mother of three sons. Anna's first two novels were published by Patrician Press and her third novel will be published in 2020 by Bluemoose. Anna is currently editing her fourth novel. She also writes poems, short stories, flash fiction, features and reviews for various publications.

Anna Johnson is an editor, book artist and bag maker. After teaching in London secondary schools, she worked in children's publishing, then took time out to have a family. She returned to academia to complete an MA in Book Art & Design. Since then, she has worked as a teacher and editor on a freelance basis and also runs workshops in schools, colleges and bookshops, covering bookbinding and book making.

About the contributors

Emma Bamford is a journalist and currently studying for an MA in Creative Writing at UEA.

Ivana Bartoletti is a privacy and data protection professional, and chairs the Fabian Women's Network.

M W Bewick is a poet and publisher at Dunlin Press.

Wersha Bharadwa is a writer, playwright, journalist and lecturer.

Mark Brayley is a poet and novelist and poetry editor at Patrician Press.

Catherine Coldstream is a poet, currently studying for a PhD at Goldsmiths.

Guy de Cruz is a musician and lyricist.

Peter Fullagar, a former teacher, is now a writer and editor. His first book was published in 2018.

J L Hall is a prizewinning Scottish novelist. She also writes short-fiction and essays.

Sam Jordison is publisher at Galley Beggar Press, a writer and Guardian book page contributor.

Emma Kittle-Pey is a writer and teacher, currently studying for a PhD in Creative Writing at the University of Essex.

Petra McQueen is a writer and teacher and Katy Wimhurst is a writer.

Chantal Mouffe is professor of political theory at the University of Westminster.

Suzy Norman is a writer, actor and artist, and formerly a journalist.

Steven O'Brien is editor of The London Magazine.

Jules Pretty OBE is a writer and Professor of Environment and Society at the University of Essex.

Mazin Qumsiyeh is Professor at the Palestine Institute of Biodiversity, Bethlehem University and Founder/Director of the Palestine Museum of Natural History.

Martin Reed is a writer, poet, stand-up and performance artist.

Robert Ronsson is a full-time writer and working on his fourth novel.

Sean Seeger is a lecturer in literature at the University of Essex.

Justine Sless is an award winning writer, comedian and creative director of Melbourne Jewish Comedy Festival.

Elisa Marcella Webb is studying for a PhD in Creative Writing at Kingston University.

Patrick Wright is a writer, broadcaster and academic in the fields of cultural studies and cultural history.

Further reading

David Andress *Cultural Dementia* Head Of Zeus (2018)

Kwame Anthony Appiah *The Honor Code: How Moral Revolutions Happen* W. W. Norton & Company (2011)

Kwame Anthony Appiah *The lies that bind: Rethinking identity* Profile (2018)

Ronald Bailey *The End of Doom* Thomas Dunne Books (2015)

John Bargh *Before You Know It; The Unconscious Reasons We Do What We Do* Penguin Random (2018)

Anthony Barnett *The Lure of Greatness: England's Brexit and America's Trump* Unbound (2017)

Stewart Brand *Whole Earth Discipline* Atlantic Books (2010)

Oliver Bullough *Moneyland: Why Thieves & Crooks Now Rule The World & How to Take It Back* Profile Books (2018)

Sam Byers *Perfidious Albion* Faber & Faber (2018)

Sarah Churchwell *Behold, America* Bloomsbury (2018)

Hillary Clinton *What Happened* Simon & Schuster (2017)

Michael D'Antonio and Peter Eisner *The Shadow President...* Macmillan USA (2018)

Ruth DeFries *The Big Ratchet: How Humanity Thrives in the Face of Natural Crisis* Basic Books (2014)

Carol Ann Duffy *Sincerity* Picador (2018)

Louise Erdrich *Future Home of the Living God* Corsair (2018)

Ronan Farrow *War on Peace* William Collins (2018)

Joshua Goldstein *Winning the War on War* Plume (2011)

Mohsin Hamid *Exit West* Penguin (2018)

Luke Harding *Collusion: How Russia Helped Trump Win the White House* Guardian Faber (2017)

Oona Hathaway and Scott Shapiro *The Internationalists And Their Plan to Outlaw War* Penguin (2017)

Aldous Huxley *Brave New World* Vintage Classics (2007)

Michiko Kakutani *The Death of Truth* William Collins (2018)

Charles Kenny *Getting Better* Basic Books (2012)

Barbara Kingsolver *Flight Behaviour* Faber (2012)

Barbara Kingsolver *Unsheltered* Faber (2018)

Elizabeth Kolbert *The Sixth Extinction: An Unnatural History* Bloomsbury (2014)

Michael Lewis *The Fifth Risk* Penguin (2018)

Attica Locke *Bluebird, Bluebird* Serpent's Tail (2017)

Rose Macaulay *What Not* Handheld Press (2019)

Nancy MacLean *Democracy in Chains: The Deep History of the Radical Right's Stealth Plan for America* Scribe UK (2017)

Chantal Mouffe *On the Political (Thinking in Action)* Routledge (2005)

John Mueller *The Remnants of War* Cornell University Press (2013)

Joyce Carol Oates *Hazards of Time Travel* HarperCollins (2018)

Michelle Obama *Becoming* Penguin Random House (2018)

George Orwell *1984* Penguin Classics; New edition (2004)

Steven Pinker *Enlightenment Now: The Case for Reason, Science, Humanism, and Progress* Viking (2018)

Steven Radelet *The Great Surge* Simon & Shuster (2015)

Robin Robertson *The Long Take* Pan Macmillan (2018)

Marilynne Robinson *What are We Doing Here?* Virago (2018)

Hans Rosling *Factfulness* Flatiron Books (2018)

Carlo Rovelli *The Order of Time* Allen Lane (2018)

Amy Siskind *The List: A Week-by-Week Reckoning of Trump's First Year* Bloomsbury (2018)

Roy Scranton *Learning to Die in the Anthropocene; We're Doomed. Now What?* Soho Press (2018)

Will Self *Phone* Viking (2017)

Ian Sinclair *The Last London: True Fictions from an Unreal City* Oneworld (2017)

Chris D Thomas *Inheritors of the Earth: How Nature Is Thriving in an Age of Extinction* Penguin (2017)

Michael Wolff *Fire and Fury: Inside the Trump White House* Macmillan USA (2018)

Bob Woodward *Fear* Simon & Schuster (2018)

Gary Younge *Another Day in the Death of America* Guardian Faber (2016)

BV - #0044 - 280119 - C0 - 216/138/12 - PB - 9781999703066